CHEESEBURGER
SUBVERSIVE

CHEESEBURGER
SUBVERSIVE

RICHARD SCARSBROOK

THISTLEDOWN PRESS

National Library of Canada Cataloguing in Publication Data
Scarsbrook, Richard
Cheeseburger subversive / Richard Scarsbrook.
ISBN 1-894345-54-1
I. Title.
PS8587.C396C43 2003   jC813'.54   C2003-910396-X
PZ7.S32712Ch 2003

Cover photograph: Peter Lavery/Masterfile
Cover and book design by J. Forrie
Typeset by Thistledown Press Ltd.
Printed and bound in Canada

Thistledown Press Ltd.
633 Main Street
Saskatoon, Saskatchewan, S7H 0J8
www.thistledown.sk.ca

ACKNOWLEDGEMENTS

The following stories have been previously published, in different form:

"Hell On Wheels", *NeWest Review*, August/September 1996.

"Benjamin's Aliens", *Backwater Review*, September 1998 (Winner of the *Backwater Review*'s 1998 Hinterland Award for Prose).

"Cheeseburger Subversive", *Storyteller: Canada's Short Story Magazine*, Winter 1999.

"Renaissance Man" was published in significantly different form as "The History of Western Art", *Winners Circle Anthology 8*, The Canadian Authors Association, 2000.

"Tristan's Quarter", *The Harpweaver*, Summer, 2000 (Second Place, The New Century Writer Awards 1999 , Short Fiction Category).

The poem "Invitation," which appears in "Thank You, Quentin Alvinstock," was originally published in the author's poetry chapbook *Guessing at Madeline* (Cranberry Tree Press, 1998).

Thistledown Press gratefully acknowledges the financial assistance of the Canada Council for the Arts, the Saskatchewan Arts Board, and the Government of Canada through the Book Publishing Industry Development Program for its publishing program.

CONTENTS

Lawn Boy
(Grade seven)

Summer vacation is here, and my dad sees the other boys in our subdivision neighbourhood emulating their fathers in manly ways. While our backyard neighbour, Mr. Potzo, tinkers with the engine in his car and curses in Italian, his son, Enzo Jr., tightens the brake calipers on his bike and curses in English. The neighbour to our left, Mr. Denney, plays garage-door goalie while his son Tommy slaps a street hockey ball at him. Across the street, Mr. Cobb slouches shirtless on a lawn chair on his porch, a beer bottle perched on his pumpkin-sized belly. He screams at his wife to bring him another beer, and his boy, Danny, who lounges beside his father, barks, "Yeah, Ma! And I wanna Coke!"

My father and I don't play driveway hockey together, nor do we work on mechanical things, nor do we abuse my mother as a father and son team, so Dad is beginning to worry that perhaps he isn't raising a well-rounded boy. As a high school teacher, he is concerned that when I enter grade nine there will be a very real danger of me getting my ass kicked frequently by hormone-addled goons.

So, Dad is doing the only thing he can think of to put me in contact with the world of real manhood: he is introducing me to our lawn mower.

At first, it doesn't seem like a bad idea to me. Since our house is built beside a steep, grass-covered hill, which is pretty difficult to keep trimmed with a push mower, Dad had recently dusted the cobwebs off his wallet and purchased a second-hand lawn tractor. As I am not yet old enough to pilot a fighter jet or race a powerboat or even push the redline on Mom's Honda Civic, I figure that our riding mower is the only kind of engine-powered excitement I'm going to get any time soon. As such, I have agreed to take on the responsibility of mowing the grounds of the Sifter estate — not that my compliance really makes any difference to my dad.

Dad throws open the garage door and the bright summer daylight floods over the mower's hood, making it glow greenish yellow like a captured alien vessel. As it turns out, an alien spaceship might be easier for a human to get running. It requires the skills of a mechanical engineer and the magic of a shaman to coax the old beast to life, neither of which are dominant traits in my English teacher father. I watch earnestly as Dad does a strange ritual dance around the rickety old lawn tractor, rapping on the fuel line with his knuckles, pinching wires together with one hand while pulling on the throttle cable with the other, and sticking his finger in the carburetor to keep the engine from flooding a second time.

"Hey, Sifter!" hollers Mr. Cobb from his seat on his front porch across the street. "You want me to send my *wife* over there to help you get that thing started?"

"That's okay, Chester," Dad answers back, "but thanks anyway. We've got it under control."

8

"Well, okay," Mr. Cobb brays, "I guess you teachers have got the whole summer off to get yer mowers going, eh?"

"I think he's making fun of us, Dad," I say, master of the obvious as usual.

"He's just jealous. Line workers at the pickle factory only get three weeks vacation. You just have to ignore people like him, Dak."

Dad wipes his brow, and resumes his shaman mechanic dance, until eventually the old engine starts backfiring and belching black smoke through the mostly functionless muffler.

"See?" says Dad, his forehead beaded with sweat and his forearms streaked with grease. "Nothing to it."

I nod seriously, somehow understanding that Dad's words are intended less for me than for Mr. Cobb and his son, who he imagines are snickering at him from their front porch seats.

"You have to take things like a man, Dak," Dad says in a philosophical way. "That's what it's all about."

And with that, he retires to the house to recover from the engine starting ordeal. I picture him sipping from a tall, cool glass of lemonade in front of the television with the fan blowing on his legs, while his only son sweats in the summer heat and bounces around the yard on top of Ol' Smoky.

After some grating and grinding, I eventually figure out how to put the old beast in gear and I carefully steer the lawn tractor around the perimeter of the front yard. I bang the mowing platform off the first nine fence posts on the far side of the yard, but with catlike reflexes, I manage to steer around the last one. With mathematical precision, I follow the tire tracks of each previous pass around the yard, so that not a single blade of grass will be left standing when I'm finished.

I am sitting up tall in the driver's seat, turning the steering wheel to make my triumphant final pass down the middle of the yard when Mr. Cobb wanders across the street to the edge of our lawn

"Hey, Lawn Boy!" he bellows over the sputtering engine, "while yer drivin' around in circles, ya might wanna actually turn the mower blades on and cut some grass!"

Oh. Right.

I reach down and pull the engage-mower knob. With a metallic screech, the mower blades began spinning beneath the tractor, and I yet again begin my journey around the front yard. I manage to improve my original record by dinging the fence only four times on this journey, which causes Mr. Cobb to shake his head even more fervently as he retreats back to his front porch. I am careful to keep an eye out for the dozen baby evergreens that Mom planted in the front yard, and it is only by accidental over steering that I turn two of them into mulch. Oh well. I figure that ten trees left standing out of twelve works out to more than eighty per cent, which is like getting an A grade at school. Dad will be proud of me!

Eventually, I repeat my triumphant final pass down the middle of the yard, and I steer the beast into the driveway to head to the backyard. In the neighbouring driveway, Mr. Denney and his son Tommy drop their hockey sticks and run to the other side of their yard to escape the flying driveway gravel that the spinning mower blades scatter like machine gun fire. Oops!

As the tractor rumbles onto the now enormous looking backyard lawn, I feel the eyes of every man and boy in the neighbourhood burning holes in the back of my neck. My discomfort is increased exponentially as I run over the garden hose, which gives me an unexpected and frigid enema when the water comes bursting up through the holes in the seat.

At this point, Dad comes running outside. He has been awakened from his nap by the sound of gravel blasting against the side of our house, then summoned outside by the water hissing against the window of his study. He has appeared just in time to witness my lawn mowing *coup de grace*, as I drive the tractor's right-side wheels up the steep slope that runs along one side of the backyard. I feel like one of those stunt drivers you sometimes see at county fairs who drive cars up on two wheels, and I can almost hear the crowd screaming with delight, until I realize that it's my dad who is screaming.

"Sit on the right fender before it flips over on you!" he hollers, but by the time I hear him over the roar of the broken muffler, the tractor is up on two wheels. I react exactly the opposite to the way a stunt driver would, by panicking and jerking the steering wheel back and forth. Luckily, I jump off as the tractor dumps over on its side, but less luckily, I land on top of one of Mom's beloved rose bushes.

The mower rolls over upside-down, its nearly bald tires spinning in the air like the twitching legs of fresh roadkill. Its engine coughs, sputters, then dies.

Mr. Potzo, Mr. Cobb, and Mr. Denney come running over from their yards and driveways, with their sons trailing close behind.

"Shit! You okay, Dak?" Mr. Denney asks.

I am lying on my back in the blazing sun, grass in my hair and mouth, rose bush thorns digging into my freshly irrigated ass, with every other male in the neighbourhood standing around me in a circle, looking down on me. I am *far* from okay.

"Yeah, I'm okay," I reply.

"Damn! What about the mower?" gasps Danny Cobb.

They all abandon me and form a new circle around the upside-down lawn tractor.

"Shit, Sifter," Mr. Potzo says to my dad, "it's toast."

"It'll be cheaper to buy a new one than to fix it," is Mr. Denney's analysis of the situation.

"Too bad. They don't build 'em like that anymore," Mr. Cobb sighs, with more affection in his voice than his wife likely ever hears.

While they all stand around, heads bowed, mourning the loss of the old lawn mower, I beat a hasty retreat into the house. I go into my bedroom and shut the door. I want to lie on my bed and pull the covers over my head, but the dirt and grass and little pinpoint bloodstains all over me make it impossible to do this without messing up the sheets, so I crawl under my bed instead.

Against the hardwood floor, I can feel the bruises forming on my back and elbows, but the bruises on my ego are much more painful. What's worse, one of the boys will probably tell the other boys at school about this travesty, and the story will eventually get around to Zoe Perry. God, that would be terrible. All the funny short stories and school bus bravado in the world will never compensate for this humiliation. Zoe will never be able to look at me again without laughing. I am never going back to school again!

I have almost convinced myself that I can adapt to life here amongst the dust bunnies beneath my bed, when I hear Dad coming down the hall towards my bedroom door. His footsteps are slow and sure, like those of a boss walking into an employee's office to tell him he's fired, or an executioner coming to take a condemned prisoner to the electric chair. Before I am able to scramble out from beneath the box spring, Dad enters the room.

"What on earth are you doing under there, Dak?" he asks.

"I dropped a pen under my bed," I lie.

"What do you need a pen for?"

"To write you a letter of apology," I say, thinking quickly.

"Ah, knock it off, Dak. It was an accident. I should have shown you what to do rather than leaving you to figure it out for yourself."

That, by the way, was the closest my father ever came to admitting that he might have been even slightly wrong about something.

"We'll do better next time, Dak," he says.

"Yeah," I say, "we will."

FOR SALE

1972 John Deere 110
LAWN TRACTOR
Best Offer!
(Needs Work)
Contact: Voicemail Box 74
Ask for Mr. Sifter

Invasion of the Blood Relatives
(Grade seven)

Our English teacher, Mrs. Mulvey, had given us a writing assignment to complete over the Christmas Break. "Each of you," she said, in that smooth, melodic voice of hers, "is to write about the true meaning of Christmas, as reflected in your own experiences of the season."

"I don't get it!" was Cliff Boswink's immediate response. This was usually what he said when he didn't feel like doing an assignment, which may explain why Cliff was taking grade seven English for a second time.

"Well, Cliff, what are some of the traditional things that come to mind when we think of the Christmas season?"

"Gettin' stuff!" he responded. Several of the boys sitting around him laughed, more likely to avoid getting punched at recess than due to any real hilarity in Cliff's response.

"Well, okay," sighed Mrs. Mulvey, "giving and receiving gifts is certainly a part of the Christmas holiday, but what else is there?"

Jake Bellows put up his hand. "The celebration of the birth of Jesus?" Jake suggested.

"Church is for weenies," Cliff grunted, casting a disdainful look at Jake meant to communicate that he could expect to be injured sometime during the next recess.

"Okay, then," Mrs. Mulvey continued, "what other non-religious aspects are there to the Christmas holiday?"

Zoe Perry raised her hand and offered, "Family! Everyone has family traditions. We could all write about those."

"Now *there* is a good idea!" Mrs. Mulvey beamed.

It is the first day back from the Christmas Break, and Mrs. Mulvey is asking for volunteers to read their compositions to the class. Cliff Boswink immediately jumps to his feet and says, "Me! Me!" He clears his throat, removes a crumpled page from his back pocket and reads:

"'The Meaning of Christmas,' by Cliff 'Blaster' Boswink.

"For Christmas I got a new helmet, gloves, and a tank of gas for my dirt bike, which *means* I can race around being cool a lot as soon as the snow melts. I got a new baseball bat, which *means* I can hit baseballs, rocks, and other stuff with it. I got a pellet gun, too, which *means . . .*"

Mrs. Mulvey interrupts him at this point, because many of the boys are now giggling, and she doesn't want things to get out of control.

"Yes, thank you, Cliff," she says, and I think she would add the words "you moron" if teachers were actually allowed to say what they're thinking. "We get the idea. A very literal interpretation of the assignment, to be sure. Now, would anyone else like to share what they wrote? How about you, Dak?"

Follow Cliff Boswink? Does she think I'm suicidal?

"Um, no, that's okay," I reply.

"Come on, Dak," says Zoe Perry, "your stories are funny!"

She bats her eyelashes at me, and I am momentarily mesmerized by those big brown eyes of hers. I think Zoe is the prettiest, nicest girl I've ever seen, but of course, I'm not stupid enough to let anyone else know about this — particularly not Zoe! Nevertheless, there is something about impressing Zoe Perry which makes me feel a little bigger and stronger than usual, which is enough to make me rise to my feet and begin reading, even if it means upstaging Cliff Boswink, and risking potential injury.

"This is called 'Invasion of the Blood Relatives,'" I say, "and it goes like this:"

In most households throughout suburbia, Christmas morning is a warm and happy family affair. Inside the cluttered split-level in which I grew up, the first few hours of December the twenty-fifth count among the happiest moments of my life.

My sister and I would wake up no later than five o'clock, and soaring high on a wave of hyperactive excitement, we would zoom around the living room, hollering and bumping into things, until our raccoon-eyed parents finally emerged from beneath their warm blankets. Occasionally, they made us suffer in anticipation until as late as six o'clock; even a minute longer than this usually resulted in my sister and me actually tugging them onto the cold floor and out into the hall. Mom and Dad were always really good sports about this, and although they always put on a great show of acting cranky and tired as they plodded down the stairs in their housecoats, I know that they were secretly delighted to see us in this annual state of euphoria.

My sister Charlotte was (and still is) three years younger than me, and was therefore granted the age-old youngest sibling's privilege of looting the first stocking. After she carefully examined each treat and trinket contained therein in a slow, deliberate way that nearly caused me to explode into conniptions of anticipation, I was finally allowed to look into the contents of my own stocking. I always got great stuff like Oh Henry bars, toy cars, and a whole book full of Lifesavers candies. My dad's stocking, on the other hand, always contained boring stuff like Bic razors, socks, and shampoo. I resolved right then and there to never become a dad.

Mom always insisted on pilfering her own stocking last. It nearly always contained a bottle of aspirin, with a little tag attached, which read, "For later, when The Cousins arrive." This little gift from Old Saint Nick never failed to amuse Mom and Dad. We all sat in a tight little family circle and laughed about this strange gift.

As the saying goes, however, all good things must come to an end. Our Christmas morning bliss was traditionally shattered with one simple line from our mother:

"Okay, kids," she would say, trying to mask the message of doom behind a cheery voice, "it's time to get ready for The Cousins!"

Sometimes Dad would whisper to us, under his breath, "Remember to hide any new toys that you don't want broken!"

Often Mom would hear him, and she would pretend to scold, "Arthur! What a thing to say about your blood relatives!"

By the time I was seven-years-old, I had become a great fan of vampire comic books (which I had to read over at my friend Mickey's because Mom and Dad were convinced that there was a verifiable link between comic books and illiteracy). If vampire comic books had taught me anything, it was that anything involving blood was to be avoided and feared; the annual invasion of our moderately peaceful household by our "blood relatives" had convinced me beyond a shadow of a doubt that those vampire books were absolutely correct.

After inhaling a quick breakfast, our household went into red alert mode — Mom did the dishes and gave the kitchen and bathroom floors a quick waxing while Dad brought in wood for the fireplace. My sister and I were invariably assigned to clean-your-room-and-stay-out-of-the-way duty.

While our parents whisked around like housekeeping elves, I set to work stockpiling our new Christmas toys under Dad's workbench in the basement where they would hopefully not be found by our Yuletide invaders. My sister assumed her annual duty which was to sit and monitor the upstairs window for early signs of the impending invasion. As soon as she heard the unmistakable rumble of one of Uncle Bob's botched do-it-yourself-for-less muffler jobs, she would shriek, "They're here! They're here!"

As she called out these words, my sister's voice, which was quiet and subdued on every other day of the year, had the startling effect of an air-raid siren. At her call we would all drop whatever we were doing and line up together at the back door, wearing smiles in the face of adversity.

At this point in the story, I could recount to you any one of a startling number of Yuletide disasters instigated by my tornado-like cousins. I could tell you about the year that one of them lit the Christmas tree on fire by accidentally spilling Christmas brandy on one of the branches and then *accidentally* holding a lit Christmas candle under the same branch for several minutes.

I could tell you about the time one of the older cousins challenged his brother to an eggnog-drinking contest, which resulted in some gravity-defying projectile vomiting and a unique stench which lingered for weeks after the holiday was over.

I could tell hundreds of stories like these, but just so things don't get too grisly for you, I will concentrate on one Christmas Day in particular. I was nine-years-old at the time but I can still recall the day with perfect clarity as if it were a news-reel playing inside my head.

They crash through the door and we brace ourselves. Their definition of talking is what we conservatively define as screaming. The extraordinary volume is compounded tenfold by the fact that they all "talk" at once.

They thunder into the kitchen. They have accidentally forgotten to remove their boots and they cut a quick path of mucky destruction across Mom's freshly waxed floor.

"Oh, my!" giggles my aunt as Mom scurries for a mop. "Look at the mess we've made of your lovely floor!"

A couple of the older kids take this as a cue to remove their boots; the younger ones do not bother. They figure the damage is already done.

My aunt is busy explaining that they have brought a bottle of liquor in lieu of a gift for my father, since they were absolutely horrified to discover at the last moment that the very, very, very expensive sweater they bought for him was accidentally seven sizes too large. So instead, they brought a forty-ounce bottle of rum. My father, incidentally, does not drink rum — but, *coincidentally*, it happens to be my aunt's favourite.

My mother nods complacently, knowing well that my aunt will have personally consumed the contents of the bottle before the last gift is unwrapped. This way she will "not feel so well" when it comes time to do the dishes. Sudden illnesses during cleanup time has become something of a holiday tradition with The Cousins.

While the two oldest cousins, Billy and Bart, pass the time by poking each other's eyes with their fingers, cousin Bruce, who is (chronologically) the same age as I am, waddles up to where I have been cowering behind my father. At first I fear that he has been watching his older brothers, and that his finger is going to find its way into my eye. I am relieved when all he does is talk.

"Whadja git fer Chrissmas, Dak?" he snorts. (He quite literally snorts — his nose is running like a broken dam).

"D'ja git any good toys? Got anything we kin play with?"

I recall Dad's annual advice, and respond appropriately.

"Uh, no, mostly clothes, actually. Just got stuff I needed this year, like some gloves, and a pair of jeans, and a scarf ... "

Bruce is uninterested in gloves and jeans and scarves, perhaps because they cannot be smashed by dropping them down the stairs. From his pocket he produces a large toy car which is made of what appears to be indestructible space-age metal. Even the wheels are made of metal! Perhaps old Santa was aware of Bruce's propensity for accidentally destroying things ...

Despite the apparent sturdiness of the toy, I have faith in cousin Bruce's abilities. The toy car will be completely dismembered before the day is over.

"Listen, Dak," he snorts again, "my car makes real race car noises when you drive it!"

He frantically rubs the car's metal wheels back and forth across the surface of the kitchen table. The car succeeds in making a feeble whirring noise; it also leaves behind a series of deep parallel gouges in the tabletop.

"Why don't you all come into the living room and sit down?" says Dad cheerfully — pretending not to notice that Bruce is busy accelerating the forces of erosion upon the kitchen table. None of The Cousins seem to hear Dad, though. They are too busy poking, hollering, and destroying.

The two youngest cousins, Adrienne and Amelia, are whining to their mother. Whining happens to be their favourite pastime, and, indeed, they have become seasoned veterans over the years. I have noticed that they are able to extract practically anything they want from their mother with this incessant and vociferous fussing. I have heard my dad say to my mom that Adrienne and Amelia will someday grow up to be professional government lobbyists.

"Mamma! Mamma! We're hungry! We're starving! Oh, Mamma, we're dying of starvation! Pleeeee-eeeee-eeease!"

After a few minutes of intense, uninterrupted screeching, my aunt reaches into her purse and produces two candy bars to shut them up until one of them thinks of something else that they are suffering without.

All of this happens within the first five minutes of their visit.

Feebly, my dad tries again.

"Hey, everybody!" he calls out with as much holiday spirit as he can muster, "how about we all get together in the living room!"

His words fall on deaf ears of course, because The Cousins' fickle attention has turned to the poking match between Billy and Bruce, which has now escalated into a full-scale, fist-swinging brawl. They are on the floor, and have rolled into the backroom, hitting and kicking and screaming and crying. Most of the kicks and punches fail to reach their intended targets, and as a result, a hanging plant suddenly ceases to hang, our cat's food dish is emptied of food, and the coat tree falls, leaving Mom's dress-up coat sprawled in a murky pool of boot-slush.

Uncle Bob, who thinks of himself as the United Nations Security Council of The Cousins' family world, is quick to react to the crisis. He rolls up his sleeves and grabs the boys by their collars, one in each hand.

"So, you wanna fight, 'n wreck everybody's Christmas, eh? Well, if you wanna fight, fight outside!"

Wearing the face of a madman, Uncle Bob kicks open the back door and hurls Billy and Bart into the snow and locks the door. The two of them lie where they land, half-buried in a snowdrift, tears freezing on their faces, steaming wet socks dangling awkwardly from their toes. It does not occur to Uncle Bob that the two boys are probably already quite humiliated, because he hollers something else, which I can hardly believe:

"You two aren't comin' in until you kiss an' make up! And it's gotta be on the lips!"

Billy and Bart look at each other in disbelief, as do my mother and my father, and my sister and myself. The other three cousins simply proceed with their ordinary business of creating noise and wrecking valuables. They are no longer interested in Billy and Bart; they have seen this sort of thing plenty of times.

"Go on, boys," yells Uncle Bob, with what sounds like malicious satisfaction, "kiss 'n make up!"

Faced with this gruesome prospect, Billy tugs off one of his sopping socks, and slaps Bart in the face with it, thus starting a violent chain reaction which sends both boys rolling across the snow-padded yard in a writhing, kicking, punching, swearing mass.

Uncle Bob turns away from the door grinning.

"Hah! Glad I'm not raisin' no sissies!" he barks, slapping my dad on the back a little more heartily than necessary and glancing over at me with an expression that suggests that my father is raising a sissy.

"Our father only raised real men, eh, brother?" He pounds my father on the back again, and for just the briefest moment, Dad forgets to look holiday happy.

"He also managed to raise at least one asshole," he mumbles to himself. Then, in the name of Christmas spirit, Dad manages to regain a false expression of cheer.

"Let's all go to the living room, okay?"

This time it is more a demand than a request, and everybody follows. Mom, fearing that the boys might freeze solid before the fight is over, discreetly unlocks the back door as she leaves the kitchen.

We all troop into the living room. Luckily, Mom has filled every available table and bench with trays of cookies, cakes, tarts, sausages and cheese, pickles, and her holiday specialty, chocolate crepes. The food distracts cousin Bruce long enough that he momentarily forgets about wrecking anything in the living room with his scrape-o-matic toy car.

My aunt drops two bags of discount-brand potato chips onto one of the tables and announces that she has added her share to the pile of Christmas goodies. She says this just before Grandma enters the room — possibly so Grandma will think my aunt actually baked some of the goodies.

Grandma nestles herself into the sofa and says, "What? Did you bring the chips?"

I like my Grandma. She's a smart cookie. In the confusion, I hadn't even noticed her until now.

"How was your trip with The Cousins, Grandma?" I ask innocently, already knowing the true answer.

"It has made me glad that I never ran away to join the circus when I was a little girl. Circus life isn't for Grandma."

Amelia and Adrienne each take a bite out of the two biggest chocolate crepes, holding them in such a way that most of the chocolate filling is destined to leak all over their clothing.

"Ohhh! Mama! I don't like these! They're yucky! They're yucky! Ohhhhh!"

"Ewwww! I got it on me! Ewwww! Oh, yuck!"

"Well, don't eat 'em, then. Put 'em on the table!"

The girls do as they are told and slap the crepes down onto the one spot on the table which is not protected by a tray or festive doily. Perhaps they have subconsciously decided that if Bruce is not going to do his job of wrecking valuables, then they will have to do it for him. Chocolate sauce leaks out all over the table and drips onto the carpet.

My aunt has only been seated for a second or two when she springs up and loudly asks if she can make anyone a drink, which means that she is ready to start emptying that bottle of rum into herself. Since it isn't even noon yet, Mom and Dad decline. My uncle agrees to a drink, as he usually does, and instructs his wife to search our cupboards for "the good stuff." Dad usually hides "the good stuff" since it has a tendency to suddenly evaporate during this particular day each year.

This year, though, Dad has hidden it in the garage, and my aunt is unable to sniff it out. Thus, my uncle is forced to settle for a specially purchased bottle of "the cheap stuff," which is empty by the time they leave. A week later, though, we notice that somebody has broken the seal on the souvenir bottle of Jamaican White Rum that Mom and Dad brought back from their honeymoon. By some freak twist of physics, the rum has somehow been changed into tap water!

Grandma, when she thinks that nobody is looking, reaches behind her ear and turns off her hearing aid. If anyone looks in her direction, she will smile sweetly and nod. This results in the delivery of a number of weakly mixed drinks, courtesy of my aunt, as well as hushed comments from my uncle implying that Grandma might be "losing her marbles". I know better than my uncle does, though, and I find myself wishing that I, too, had a volume control on my hearing. Like I said, Grandma is pretty smart.

Amelia and Adrienne finally stop whining about the chocolate crepes, but they are scarcely able to draw another breath before they have found more ammunition for their flame-thrower mouths.

"Presents!" they screech. "We wanna open our presents!"

They begin to chant, like rowdy spectators at a football game.

"Pre-sents! Pre-sents!"

Cousin Bruce has re-discovered his toy car and is attempting to start an electrical fire by "driving" it back and forth over the electrical cord leading to the Christmas tree lights. Luckily, he is distracted by the girls' shouting, and decides to join in. Grandma sits and smiles placidly, and Mom and Dad grin absently, like shock victims.

My uncle suddenly feels philosophical, and decides to share a little of his wisdom with his shouting children.

"Ya know, kids, if you wanna get anything outta this crazy world we live in, ya gotta scream a lot louder than that. The squeaky wheel gets the grease, so they say."

Naturally, Amelia, Adrienne, and Bruce start screeching like industrial turbines, loud enough to summon Bart and Billy, who saunter into the room dripping wet. They join in the shouting, which actually causes the Christmas tree to shake. My dad decides to put a stop to it before ornaments start falling from the tree and bouncing on the floor. (I say bouncing rather than shattering because after the ornament fight between Billy and Bart the previous year, Mom and Dad decided that although plastic was less attractive than glass, it was also less dangerous).

"Okay!" Dad hollers, while still trying to maintain a festive holiday tone of voice. "Okay! We'll open the presents now!"

"Yaaaaaaaaaaaaay!" comes the thundering response from the five cousins. Surprisingly, only one ornament falls.

The din fades to "talking", and the overwhelmed, achy sensation in my head subsides long enough for me to notice that a thick stream of blood is trickling from Billy's left nostril; apparently, Bart won the fight. His other nostril is equally saturated, but with a glob of mucus, much like his younger brother Bruce had displayed earlier. Perhaps the ability to manufacture gallons of nose goop is a genetic trait that Bruce and Billy share.

Bruce, who is normally as observant as a moss-covered boulder, immediately notices Billy's nose and shrieks, "Hey! Look, everybody! Billy's nose is spouting the Christmas colours — red and green!"

All of the kids laugh riotously at this — even I laugh. Give me a break — I'm nine-years-old, okay? To me, boogers are still a source of entertainment.

Still laughing, we all tear into our presents.

I have been given a sweatshirt which unlike in previous years, actually fits me. I am overjoyed, and I thank my aunt and uncle profusely. Then, in a taunting tone of voice, Bruce informs me that the sweatshirt was actually one of his Christmas presents, but it turned out to be too small for him so it was re-wrapped and given to me.

"I guess you're jus' not as big 'n strong as me, huh?" Bruce sputters.

In the interests of riot prevention, I decide to concede this point rather than punching Bruce in his big 'n strong nose. I find myself wondering whether Bruce would actually notice the difference if his brain suddenly fell out on the floor.

My parents have put careful consideration into the gifts they have wrapped for The Cousins. For the younger ones, Mom and Dad have purchased toys that conform to the following specifications: None of them can be easily broken, none of them can be used as life-threatening weapons, and none of them make noise. Since the two oldest cousins have evolved to the point where they are capable of turning any solid object into a dangerous weapon, my parents have given them cash; the worst damage they can inflict upon each other with a twenty dollar bill is maybe a paper cut or two.

The Cousins soon toss aside the toys, which are judged too boring since they bear no resemblance to missiles or guns. Thus, they begin their annual stampede around our house, each on his or her own special seek-and-destroy mission. Within minutes, the two eldest boys have dismembered one of Charlotte's dolls. Fortunately, it was a decoy placed by my crafty little sister; her new doll remained safely hidden in the basement.

The two youngest cousins waste no time in finding my stash of Christmas candy, and they have gobbled it all up before I can find where they're hiding. Luckily, my real Christmas candy is hidden away, guarded by my sister's new doll. The stuff devoured by The Cousins is old Halloween candy that I saved especially for their visit; the girls are not deterred by the fact that the candies are wrapped in black and orange paper which is adorned with ghosts and goblins. I can't believe they have actually eaten it all without breaking any teeth. Hopefully, they will wait until they're in their car before they decide to throw up.

Meanwhile, Billy is standing in the living room wailing, great big tears rolling down his cheeks. I am a little suspicious of this — normally a steamroller would have to drive over Billy's head to make his eyes water. Under normal circumstances, he is far too stunned to be this sensitive about anything. Naturally, I wonder what's going on.

"Oh, Auntie!" he cries to my mother, "I lost the money you gave me! Oh, no! Now I don't have a Christmas present! Oh, no! Christmas is ruined!"

Oh, the drama that follows! All the kids scurry about the house looking for Billy's lost money — not really out of particular love for Billy, but because Mom has promised a reward of two dollars to whoever returns the money. I suppose she would rather part with the reward money than listen to Billy bellow all afternoon.

The Cousins scour most of the house, but the twenty-dollar bill does not turn up.

"Hey!" shouts Amelia, "maybe the money got loose and floated into the basement!"

My sister and I look at each other in terror. What if they find our new toys down there! A scene of sheer destruction enters my imagination, and I begin to sweat.

I'm going to have to think fast. I have to figure out where that twenty is before The Cousins decide to look in the basement.

In a panic, I shout, "Hey! Maybe the money is still in your pants! Did you check all of your pockets, Billy?"

Billy's face suddenly flushes.

"Are you accusing me of trying to get an extra twenty bucks out of Auntie?" He sounds more angry than hurt.

"Uh, no, just, um, maybe it's stuck in one of your pockets. . ."

Billy refuses to dig into his pockets. So my uncle holds him down on the floor and does it for him. And wonder of wonders, the twenty-dollar bill has been in Billy's pocket the entire time!

"Nice try, Billy," grumbles my aunt, as she retreats to the kitchen to mix yet another drink.

Billy brushes past me.

"Better not leave the living room, Twerp, cause I'm gonna punch ya in the head for what you just did to me."

He says this just quietly enough so that none of the adults can hear.

What a swell kid. I am willing to bet a year's allowance that Billy will be the first member of our family to spend time in a maximum-security prison. Luckily, by the time dinner is ready, I have managed to remain free of injuries.

Aside from an unusual amount of airborne food, dinnertime passes without serious incident. Sure, there is a lot of whining and yelling, spiced with the traditional fake burping and farting that The Cousins seem to find endlessly entertaining, but unlike certain years past, nobody has to be hospitalized. My aunt has to lie down after dinner (due to a sudden bout of unexplained dizziness) and yet again, she misses out on helping with the dishes.

Fortunately, the television is on. The Cousins, full of weighty food, sit on the floor, mesmerized, motionless, practically catatonic. It is a rare moment during which nothing is destroyed and nobody is punching or kicking anyone. Peace on Earth and Goodwill Towards All, indeed.

When the remaining unbroken presents have been stowed away in my uncle's station wagon, The Cousins trudge away to the car. Without making eye contact, Billy punches my shoulder on his way to the door. The way he sees it, I have cost him twenty dollars. I decide not to say anything about the punch; any interpersonal conflict might set back their departure time.

Before the car's engine is even started, my aunt falls asleep in the front seat. In the back, Billy and Bart have returned to their natural state of existence, which means that they are vigorously punching each other. The doors slam shut, the car careens its way along our laneway, and an eerie silence follows. We wave goodbye as the car vanishes from sight.

Each year, as the taillights of the car full of cousins disappears down the road, we all stand in the doorway and smile, despite our ringing ears. And our smiles are real. In front of the storm door window that whistles softly from the wind, we look out across the hushed, snow-covered fields and heave a collective sigh.

We stand, sharing the warmth and quiet. I even hug my sister. My parents put their arms around each other, with my sister and I wedged in between. It's a family hug, the best kind there is.

When I finish reading my story, Mrs. Mulvey smiles broadly. Everyone in the classroom applauds, except for Cliff Boswink, who lets out a big, fake yawn to express to his followers how boring he found the entire story. Who cares. How could I when for the past fifteen minutes Zoe Perry has been looking right at me with those big brown eyes, listening to every word I've said.

Hell on Wheels

(Grade seven)

There is a feeling of tension this morning on Faireville Board of Education Bus #16. There is almost no talking in the back seats, and the snapping of gum is more focused and intense than usual. None of us is sure whether the rumours are true, that the world is going to end at exactly 8:35 this morning.

The little kids are having a good old time up there in the front of the bus, insulated by youth, oblivious to the shadow that hangs over us. They chatter to themselves, innocent and unsuspecting, like squirrels just before being shot at by wiry Older Boys with BB guns.

I'm an Older Boy. That's me at the back of the bus. I am in the seventh grade. In the seventh grade, you can no longer ignore scary things by simply believing in magic kingdoms and happy endings the way little kids do.

Grade seven does have its rewards, though. Those of us who survive this long are granted special privileges; one is a reserved seat at the back of the school bus. I don't get to sit in an aisle seat, however; only grade eights have graduated to this esteemed position. Aisle seats are more conducive to socializing than window seats, and are thus highly coveted property (even though socializing, as we know it, consists of boys making rude noises and the girls ignoring us). When one boy moves in on another's bus-turf, it usually results in a well-publicized after-school fist fight, or, at the very least, a good four-letter-word shouting match.

Without actually being able to put names to the concepts, we have learned about the Right to Property, the Conflict Theory of Society, and the Survival of the Fittest; not from books but from experience. We are Adults-In-Training.

The boys closely guard the bus seats because there are only two older girls on our route. They usually sit together, which makes it difficult for the boys to attain strategic socializing positions. The girls are Amanda Randall, who is in grade eight, and her grade seven subordinate, Zoe Perry. All of the boys desire their attention although none of us is sure exactly why.

Usually, Zoe sits in front of me. I like Zoe a lot, but I know that to reveal this would result in social crucifixion at the hands of the other boys. So I say nothing.

Amanda Randall usually sits with Zoe, unless Zoe has committed some Atrocity of Uncool such as skipping rope or listening to last year's music. In such cases of social uncouth, Zoe loses her apprentice status for a couple of days and must sit with me instead of Amanda. Amanda does not see such ostracism as cruelty; she is simply trying to teach Zoe to deserve her acceptance.

Because Amanda is in grade eight, she rarely speaks to me. Acknowledging the existence of a boy younger than herself would be in violation of the laws of grade eight femininity. I understand this; for Amanda to be accused of consorting with a grade seven boy would be like me getting caught playing with toy cars. It would mean social death.

Of course, Amanda is allowed to bend the rules when she needs help with her math problems. I have been "accelerated" to grade eight math classes, so Amanda figures that I qualify as an honorary grade eight as long as we are discussing math and nothing else. I am what they term "gifted" when it comes to mathematics, although I don't see it as much of a gift; I would rather be tall and muscular with nice clothes and a lucrative allowance. I would rather look and dress like Cliff Boswink, the lone grade eight boy on our bus, although I find his personality as pleasant as a pulled groin.

I do get some conciliatory pleasure from the fact that it makes Cliff jealous when Amanda asks me to do her math homework for her. Every time Amanda passes me her math book, Cliff launches into a loud description of his latest dirt bike adventure. "Vroom! Vroooooom! Right over the ditch! Ka-boom! I land on the other side!" he brags loudly, amid choruses of admiration from the younger boys on the bus. Amanda, however, is not particularly impressed, and remains focused on her math. Cliff's jealousy pleases me, and it helps me ignore that Amanda is using me.

Both Amanda and Zoe have achieved bump status, which means that their breasts have grown large enough to warrant brassieres. They go to health classes separate from the boys. In our own all-boy health classes, we have each been given a pamphlet called *You and Your Privates*, which informs us that we should feel comfortable about our privates (sensitively referred to as our little weenies by our gym teacher, Mr. Zell). Just in case we aren't one-hundred-per-cent comfortable though, Mr. Zell has placed a question box at the front of the classroom. The box is there to ensure anonymity, we have been told, but I suspect that the box may also provide a convenient way for Mr. Zell to edit out any questions he feels are "inappropriate."

To be quite honest, none of us boys is really very interested in reading about our own "privates," since there is nothing very private about them. Each of us has had them for as long as we can remember, and we have seen many others hanging around in the locker room of the community swimming pool. What we would really like to read are the pink pamphlets that the girls carry out of their health classes, ones that quickly disappear into the recesses of their purses, never to be seen by male eyes. The only thing we know for certain is that the girls' "privates" are much more private than ours.

I have taken it upon myself to do some research on the subject by smuggling several old copies of *Playboy* from my uncle Paul's garage. Now there are at least a dozen new words floating around in my head, dark and mysterious. I worry that I might be missing some genetic encoding, some built-in instinct about this sex stuff. Nobody else appears to be very concerned about it.

When I am not engaged in some sort of shoulder-punching activity with the other boys, I spend most of my time thinking about girls, often with physically uncomfortable results which I hope nobody will notice when I stand. At home, my father laughs and tells me that I have "girls on the brain." Sometimes I think the condition could be fatal.

Today is different, though. I am not thinking about girls (at least not very much). Very little socializing is taking place. The back of the bus is strangely quiet.

From my own spot in the back left corner, I can see the waxed dome of old Mr. Overhill's bald spot reflected in the large mirror that hangs above the windshield. As you would expect from a squadron of sharp twelve and thirteen-year-old minds, we have given Mr. Overhill the clever nickname, "Old Over-the-Hill," since he is well over forty. He reminds us periodically of his elderly stature by driving the bus over curbs and potholes. We forgive him for this tendency, since buses probably hadn't been invented when Old Over-the-hill was still in his formative years. It does not occur to us that Mr. Overhill derives some sort of sadistic thrill from bouncing the crap out of his chatty, hyperactive passengers.

Even Old Over-the-Hill is acting differently today. He is not glancing up into his surveillance mirror, nor is he screaming at us to sit down, to be quiet, or to stop throwing things. Even he, the bastion of adult predictability, is acting as if the rumours might be true.

Old Over-the-Hill glances down at his watch, and I find myself doing the same. Some of the other kids are asking each other for the time. A few are synchronizing their watches. It is 8:27 AM.

Cliff Boswink makes a concerted effort to appear unconcerned. He folds his arms across his intimidating chest muscles, and rolls his eyes towards the peeling pus-green speckle paint on the ceiling.

"Fer cryin' out loud, Sifter," he brays, whacking me on the back, "you look like yer about ta leave Hershey-squirts in yer Mr. Briefs!"

This is the type of brashness that everyone has come to expect from Cliff Boswink. Cliff is the self-declared coolest guy in all of Faireville Elementary School. So far, nobody has challenged him for the title, because Cliff has a reputation for punching people at the slightest provocation.

The girls sometimes buy him potato chips at lunchtime as symbols of their undying devotion. He always takes the chips and says something unbelievably suave and sophisticated like, "bring me the barbecue kind next time, 'kay." Cliff is so cool that he has even made up his own nickname; he expects us to refer to him as "Blaster" Boswink. This is how *cool* Cliff is.

Jake Bellows, the other grade seven boy on the bus, shifts his substantial weight in the seat, and the green vinyl makes a sound like a balloon leaking.

"Whatsa matter, Jakey?" winks Cliff. "You shit yerself?"

"Shit, no, Blaster!" chatters Jake, "I ain't worried 'bout nothin'!"

Under normal circumstances, Jake would have said something like, "Why, no, Cliff, I'm not worried about anything." Jake Bellows has a professor for a father and a lawyer for a mother; in the Bellowses' household, the use of proper English is considered as important as breathing. When you're talking to someone as cool as Cliff, though, a different sort of lingo is required. It is one of the unwritten laws of coolness: Never act smarter than anyone more cool than yourself. Anyone who breaks this rule runs the risk of being called a Smartass, an Einstein, a Browner, or worst of all, a Geek. And everyone knows that geeks are apt to be punched. Often.

"There ain't nothin' to be worried about," Jake repeats, as if he needs to convince himself of the fact.

"Good," croaks Cliff, "ain't nothin' to be worried about. It's just a stupid hoax."

Of course, it's just a hoax. No one among us really believes what that guy on TV said, even though he was on all of the talk shows and even the eight o'clock news last night; everyone knows that he's wrong, he's out of his mind, he's a certifiable nutcase.

The guy on TV said that he had proof — mathematical, astronomical, and biblical proof — that the world is going to end at 8:35 this morning. We all know that he's full of crap. Even my father says so, and he should know. My father is a high school English teacher, and is used to people trying to pass absurdity off as fact.

Of course, there is absolutely *nothing* to worry about. The world is not going to end at 8:35. Despite knowing this, we are all a little edgy.

It is 8:31.

I know I am not going to die in this bus, beneath the garish green ceiling dome. Even if the world really is going to end in four minutes, I know that most of the kids sitting on this bus will go to Heaven. So there is nothing to worry about.

The rest of course will spend the rest of eternity in hell, burning and screaming, wishing they had never sinned. I know these things, because I used to go to Sunday

School. I know that everyone goes to Heaven except for the sinners. I find myself wondering whether or not it is a sin to quit going to Sunday School. The rules of sinning are a bit vague on this point; "Thou Shalt Not Be Bored By Sunday School" is not one of the Ten Commandments. At least I know the Ten Commandments, which should count for something, I hope.

I heard my father explaining the idea of hell during a telephone conversation with one of his high school English students.

"The popular conception of hell as an eternal, tortuous fire," he cheerily explained, "is *only* a literary metaphor for the torments that hell really embodies. The anguish described in the literature we have read is only what the various authors imagine it would feel like to be disinherited by God. Okay?"

I didn't quite understand what he meant by all of that, and I was not comforted by his reassuring tones. I still think of hell as a real place. The Devil is a real guy, not a metaphor or whatever my father would call him.

The Devil does not have horns, a forked tail, or a little French moustache. This much I understand. The Devil is not stitched together from red satin like a little kid's Halloween costume. The Devil *is* a man with a large chin and steel-grey eyes, wearing a black business suit, standing in front of a large door with a huge question mark painted upon it. He brays in a smarmy TV game-show announcer's voice, "And now, studio audience, please put your hands together as our next unlucky sinner steps through the mystery door into an endless barrage of previously unimagined horrors . . . " He sweeps his hand toward the door, and it swings open to the roar of morally righteous applause.

Sometimes I have nightmares like this. Fortunately, I have always awakened before stepping through the door.

Of course, I realize how silly these thoughts are. I try to shut them off. I try to think about hockey, or space ships, or about Zoe Perry, who is sitting right in front of me. I think that I'm in love with Zoe, but if I die today it won't matter much, will it? You can't fall in love in hell.

It is 8:34. I am holding my breath.

I think about how I felt when I peed my pants in the second grade. The shame was so overwhelming, I started punching myself in the stomach to give myself something less painful to focus on. Maybe hell is like approaching the door to your grade two classroom, reeking of urine and burning with shame.

Once I was playing with the sterling silver locket that had belonged to my mother's great grandmother, which I was warned to never touch. I watched with horror as it slipped through the radiator grate. Maybe hell is like never getting caught, like never confessing.

Maybe hell is like having your best friend hold your hands behind your back while everyone lines up to punch you twelve times because it's your twelfth birthday. The adults in hell just laugh about it, tell you that you must "learn to take things like a man."

Maybe hell is like being lost in the dark, and feeling that invisible eyes are watching you, even in the privacy of your own bedroom. Maybe hell is like dreaming dreams you can't stop. Maybe hell is waking up, heart racing, pyjamas wet.

The second hand on my watch seems to be slowing; I wonder if our bus is heading into a time warp. I know that these things exist; I am a faithful watcher of *Star Trek*.

It is 8:35.

The bus hits a bump, and bodies are momentarily airborne, weightless. The kids at the front scream with joy; the kids at the back just scream.

Then we all chuckle, pretending it was fun. We have passed 8:35 and none of us seem to be in hell.

"Well," says Cliff, "I told you chicken-shits there was nothin' to worry about."

He turns to me.

"See, Turd-Bird! Nothin' happened."

I have some idea why Cliff keeps calling me this name; it most certainly has to do with what my father calls an inferiority complex. This sounds like something an idiot like Cliff might have, but it doesn't make his name-calling any less humiliating.

"I don't recall saying that anything was going to happen, Cliff, you retard," is my unspoken riposte. This, of course, is what I would like to say to Cliff. I don't actually say this because I don't want to get beaten up in front of Amanda and Zoe.

"Hah! Nothin' happened! That guy on TV was full of it!" chortles Cliff. "Everything is the same as it was before."

My father has a favourite expression from Shakespeare. I decide to repeat this expression to Cliff.

"Methinks you dost protest too much." It is a safe thing to say because Cliff will certainly not understand it.

"Huh?" comes the expected response.

I notice that Zoe is listening. This knowledge makes me feel brave, and I continue.

"I think you were scared, too, Cliff."

"What the hell are you . . . ?"

I do not let him finish his sentence. Zoe is pretending to read a teen magazine but she is really listening to Cliff and I. I am feeling beyond brave now, because it has suddenly occurred to me that the fondness I feel for Zoe is being quietly returned, like a shared secret.

"And, if I were you," I say, "I'd be even *more* scared right now."

My heart is pounding in my throat because I realize I have just crossed a line. Something is going to happen, something I will not be able to stop.

"What the hell are you talkin' about?" snarls Cliff, like a confused, trapped animal. His growl scarcely conceals his confusion.

"Hell is exactly what I'm talkin' about, Cliff old pal."

Oops. He has detected that I am mocking him.

"Are you asking for a busted face, Turd-Bird?" Cliff asks. I know that he has no intention of hitting me. Not yet. He would rather let me back down voluntarily. But I won't do it this time. Something inside me has snapped.

"Maybe I know something that you don't, Cliff. Not that *that's* surprising."

Cliff puts on a tough expression for Zoe and Amanda, who are watching from the edge of their seat.

"You'd better take that back, Turd . . . "

"Let me ask you a question," I say.

The killer instinct takes over.

"How do you know that the world really *didn't* end at 8:35, Cliff?"

Cliff looks confused. Not a major surprise.

"How do you know that you haven't passed straight into hell, that the Devil isn't just fooling you into thinking you're still on the school bus? How do you know that demons aren't going to suddenly pop out and rip you to shreds, Cliff? How do you know you're not on the bus to hell?"

The tone in my voice surprises me. It is as if I have pulled the release pin out of the cylinder in the back of my head from which all the nightmares come.

Cliff is no longer sure whether or not I am joking.

"Knock it off, Turd-Bird. You're buggin' me."

"Calling me Turd-Bird is not a very intelligent thing to do right now, Cliff."

"Why not?" He rolls up his sleeve, preparing to punch.

"Why not?" I holler. "Because you don't know whether or not I'm who you think I am. Maybe the world ended two minutes ago, and now you're in hell. Tell me Cliff, am I Dak Sifter, or am I a demon in disguise?"

I look him straight in the eyes.

"Can you say that you know for *sure*?"

"Shut up, Sifter! You're a psycho!"

"Or maybe just a demon, eh? You never can tell, can you, Cliff?"

My eyes are bulging maniacally.

"Am I a demon, Cliff? What do you think?"

Cliff may actually be scared. I am frightening myself a little, because I am starting to enjoy what I am doing to him.

Amanda is watching with the fascination some people have for film footage of airplane crashes and convenience store shootings. Cliff turns to her.

"Tell Sifter he's a dickhead, Amanda."

I expect Amanda to do this, since she is one of the girls who often buys potato chips for Cliff. To my surprise, Amanda tells Cliff to grow up.

"But Cliff can't grow up if he died three minutes ago, can he?" I cackle. "He won't ever grow up!"

"You never know, do you Cliff?" Amanda says sweetly. She doesn't wish to fail grade eight for want of a passing grade in math.

"You're a bimbo, Amanda," Cliff grumbles. "You can forget about going to the movies with me again!"

Amanda, who usually wears the expression of a deer caught in a pair of car headlights, becomes enraged.

"Dead guys don't go to movies, Cliff!" she screeches like skidding tires. "You're not so cool now that you're dead, are you?"

Then, she turns to ice, rotating slowly around in her seat with her head cocked back. Wow. Girls are so good at that!

"Whoops! Bad move, Cliff!" I chirp. "But don't worry, old pal, you won't be needing girlfriends where *you're* headed . . . "

Cliff is turning red. Oh-oh! Could Cliff be losing his famous cool? I am bent on seeing this happen.

"Maybe the flames won't burn you too badly, Cliff, given that you're so cool . . . "

I feel a sharp blow against my jaw, and the back of my head bounces against the bus window.

Momentary blackness . . .

I can feel the warmth of my blood trickling into my mouth, slowly filling it. Cliff has punched me in the face. Dull pain rises from the back of my head and my lower lip throbs.

Cliff stands in the aisle, still-clenched fists hanging at his sides, and he begins to cry. Although he has punched me in the face, he is the one who's crying. Despite loosened, bloody teeth, I am grinning.

My head hardly hurts at all, relatively speaking. I have lost teeth to snowballs with rocks inside them and I have been knocked off my bicycle by biting dogs. Back when I was younger, and I went to the Special School for "gifted" kids, I got hit in the privates with a baseball bat just because I rode on a different bus than the other neighbourhood brats. So a punch in the face is nothing.

Zoe shimmies around Amanda, and squeezes into the seat beside me. She mops blood from my mouth with a Kleenex, looking admiringly worried.

"Ohmigod!" she says. "Are you okay?"

"Yeah. It's nothing."

It occurs to me at this moment that Zoe is going to grow up to be a very attractive woman.

Cliff is sitting in his seat, knees against his face, hiding. It is too late, though, and he knows it.

What will happen from this point will go something like this: Cliff will be sent down to the principal's office by the bus driver. Zoe and Amanda will be called in as witnesses, because girls are seen to be above this sort of boyish nonsense.

Of course, Amanda and Zoe will tell the principal that I did absolutely nothing to provoke such a heartless attack, and the principal will believe it. In the past, Cliff has had a tendency to be a bit too "cool" with the teachers, whereas I have been on the honour roll every year since grade one.

Cliff will pay for the broken window. He will apologize to me. He will be watched like a prison inmate for the remainder of the school year. He will probably also collect fewer potato chips at lunch. Poor Cliff.

He looks at me from across the aisle, head between his knees. He would like to apologize for hitting me, if only to save his own skin, but his residual coolness prevents this from happening.

Even though I have stopped bleeding, Zoe continues to gently rub my lip with the Kleenex.

Cliff sits and cries.

Welcome to hell, Cliff.

THE FAIREVILLE BOARD OF EDUCATION
"TEACHING TOMORROW TODAY"

OFFICIAL NOTICE OF SUSPENSION

Dear Mr. and Mrs. Boswink,

This notice is to inform you that your child/charge has been suspended from school for three days for the reasons outlined below:

_____

Cliff is suspended under Section 12 (a) of the Education Act, for "personal conduct injurious to the moral tone of the school community," specifically, the harassment and unprovoked assault of another student, while riding Bus 16 to school on Wednesday, February 11.

The incident was witnessed by the bus driver, Mr. C. Underhill, as well as by several students.

_____

The suspension will begin on <u>February 12</u>. You must accompany your child/charge to school on <u>February 15</u> at <u>9:00</u> AM for re-instatement.

Ronald J. Kells
Principal

Dogs That Lick and Dogs That Bite
(Grade eight)

I once read that the personalities of dogs tend to reflect those of their owners and vice versa, and I suppose this is true of me and my dog, Smiley. Smiley never bites, growls, or barks unnecessarily, and neither do I. He is the kind of dog who can't catch or even find a ball that is thrown to him, and I, unfortunately, am that kind of boy. All of my report cards say that I am an "earnest, polite student," and I get As in everything except physical education; if they issued report cards for dogs, Smiley's probably would look a lot like mine.

I think my father has been hoping for something a little different. After watching several old *Lassie* re-runs on TV, Dad concluded that I needed a dog, one that was noble, loyal, brave, and adventurous, in the hope that some of these traits would rub off on me. Despite the assurances of the pet store owner that Smiley would eventually grow out of his awkward, stumbling puppy gait, and would become a good guard dog and hunter with time, Smiley remains clumsy, skinny, relatively passive, and uninterested in hunting or guarding of any kind, which are traits I already have in abundance. At least both of my ears are more or less the same, whereas Smiley always has one ear sticking up and one ear lying down.

Dad knew for sure he had hit another roadblock on his journey to make a man of me when I named my new dog. Dad suggested some "good, old-fashioned dog names" like "Rex," "Rover," and "Buster," but I decided to name my fluffy new puppy Smiley, because he always looked happy. When Zoe Perry came over to see my new puppy, and declared that Smiley was an "adorable" name, Dad gave up the fight and retreated to his den to watch war movies on TV (which is probably why I got a pellet gun — which I didn't ask for — for Christmas this year). Nevertheless, since dogs prefer to pee on trees and the wheels of neighbours' cars, I, at least, have to go outdoors more often, which has convinced Dad that his mission has not been a total failure.

Despite our relative passivity as a boy-and-dog team, Smiley and I manage to have a pretty good time together. Smiley splashes in the ravine across the street while I skip stones across the shallow water. Smiley gleefully rolls around on whatever dead thing he manages to sniff out, and I usually lose my balance on a stepping-stone and end up falling into the stagnant water. That we bring the stench of the ravine home with us on a regular basis drives Mom nuts, but it makes Dad happy to see me covered in guck like a "normal" boy.

Today is a hot, kiln-fire dry summer afternoon. The ravine is dried up, so I can't skip stones, and there is nothing moist and stinky for Smiley to roll around in, so today we decide to venture past the ravine to a barren, undeveloped region that both the kids and adults in our subdivision call The Badlands. On a bright day like this one, you can stand at the edge of The Badlands and watch the heat-distorted air twist above the parched ground, and you can squint, grit your teeth, and pretend that you're Clint Eastwood in *The Good, The Bad, and the Ugly*.

The adults call it The Badlands because this hilly patch of land is unfarmed, uninhabited, and undeveloped, due to its uneven terrain, its cracked, unyielding clay ground, and the unsightliness of its scraggly weeds and mounds of industrial waste containers and windblown garbage. The neighbourhood kids call it The Badlands because it is where the notorious Bad Boys hang out.

The Bad Boys are mostly in grade nine or ten, only a couple of years older than me, but their reputations are bigger than age or size alone. Cliff Boswink, the bully of bullies at our middle school, is merely a little toadie in this gang of thugs. The Bad Boys have claimed The Badlands as their turf. It is the place where they roar around on their noisy, mufflerless dirt bikes, then stop to swear, spit, and smoke cigarettes stolen from the local convenience store. Mr. Cheung, the store's owner, has started turning a blind eye to their petty thefts. Last time he apprehended the Bad Boys, his store got spray-painted with terms like "faggot chink" and "bumfucker store."

Smiley and I peer into The Badlands from atop a hill, my elbows and knees rest against the hard ground, and Smiley sprawls on his belly like a reconnaissance agent. What we see makes my heart race with excitement.

Half a dozen dirt bikes buzz around the landscape of The Badlands like angry wasps around their hive, kicking up plumes of dust behind their spinning tires. The riders spin in cyclone circles, sound roaring into the air. The speed! The noise! The excitement! I've got to get one of these machines!

The kid on the tallest bike brings his ride to a halt in the center of a bowl-shaped indentation between the hills. He stays on top of his bike, allowing the dust to clear before he kills the machine-gun sputtering of his bike's idling motor. He tugs off his helmet, tosses it on the ground beside him, and flips the mane of sweaty hair from his face. It is Devin Orff, the undisputed leader of the Bad Boys, sitting atop his stone-dented, mud-splattered Suzuki RM 250, the sleeves of his black shirt rolled up past his shoulders to reveal wiry muscles, which he manages to flex through the simple action of inhaling from a cigarette.

One by one, the other Bad Boys park their dirt bikes in a circle around him. They ride Hondas, Yamahas, and Suzukis with 125 cc engines. I suppose Devin gets to be the leader because his bike is a little bigger and a little faster than the others. The two huge Dobermans, which nip and snarl at each other at Devin's feet, probably also help to reinforce his position of leadership. Devin kicks one of the dogs, sending it yelping around to the other side of his bike.

"Knock it off, ya damn idiots!" Devin grunts at the dogs.

"Yeah, ya stupid mutts!" adds one of Devin's toadies, who kicks at the second dog.

Devin slowly levers his long right leg over the gas tank of his dirt bike, then takes two quick strides over to the kid who has just taken a boot at the second Doberman. He stares at him for a moment, then kicks the kid's bike over on top of him. The kid jumps to his feet, brushes the dirt off his hands, inspects the scrapes on his elbows, and struggles to pull his bike up off the ground.

"What the hell did you do that for?" the toadie whines, his voice cracking like someone who wants to cry, but knows he can't.

"Chopper 'n' Slash are *my* dogs, dickwad. Only *I* get to discipline 'em. They'd better be chewin' yer *balls* off before you ever touch 'em. Get it?"

The kid looks down at his feet in the dust and says nothing.

"I asked you a question!" Devin rasps.

"Yeah, I got it," the toadie mumbles.

One of the Dobermans lifts its nose in the air, toward the spot where Smiley and I are hiding behind the hill and begins barking furiously. The second dog joins in. Smiley scampers quickly down the hill into the shelter of the ravine.

"Hey, Devin! There's somebody spyin' on us!" calls a toady.

Following my little dog's wise example, I beat it down the hill. My heart is thumping in my throat as we hastily retreat home, but it isn't just because we nearly got caught spying on the Bad Boys. The sound, speed, and motion of those motorcycles ripping around The Badlands has touched something deep inside of me, a feeling of desire unlike anything I have ever felt before. It has created inside me a need for speed, power, and motion. I want one of those dirt bikes. I *need* one.

It is night, and I am listening from the top of the stairs as Mom and Dad argue furiously over whether or not I can spend my allowance money, which I have been saving since the third grade, on a dirt bike. Dad sees his boy suddenly wanting to do something "manly" without being forced into it, while Mom envisions me being smashed into a million pieces and scattered over The Badlands.

"He'll kill himself!" Mom wails. "Motorcycles are too dangerous for boys!"

"It will teach him to be responsible and cautious," Dad counters. "Dozens of the other neighbourhood boys have got them."

"He'll get into trouble!" Mom argues.

"It'll keep him *out* of trouble," Dad reasons. "It's good, wholesome fun. He'll make new friends with the other boys who ride."

"He'll knock his teeth out or break his arm!"

"It'll be good for him. He'll improve his hand-eye coordination. He'll get more fresh air."

"He'll get hurt!"

"If he's careful, he won't."

"Yes he will!"

"No, he won't. He'll learn to respect limits."

"No, he won't. If that Evil Kneivel guy, who was a professional motorcycle rider, could break every bone in his body in a crash, Dak will break every bone in his body twice!"

"No, he won't."

"Yes, he will!"

"No, he won't."

Mom's voice shifts down a tone, the way it does when she is about to win an argument with some unassailable fact.

"Arthur, Dak can't walk across the yard without tripping. He couldn't *mow the lawn* without destroying the lawn tractor. And now you want to let him spend his *entire life's savings* on something that's almost as heavy as the lawn mower, but only has two wheels and goes *a hundred times faster*?"

Intentionally missing Mom's point, Dad replies:

"He doesn't have to spend his life savings on it. I *want* him to have it. *I'll* buy it for him."

Mom is silent. She is probably as shocked as I am. Normally, Mom practically has to hold a bazooka to Dad's head just to get him to buy himself a new pair of socks. If he is willing to fork out his own cash for my dirt bike, it's pretty clear just how much he wants me to have one.

My heart palpitates for the next two weeks as I await the delivery of my new ride. I bought some motorcycle magazines, and have begun to replace the *Star Wars* posters on my bedroom walls with pictures of dirt bikes. The anticipation is nearly killing me, but I can't ask my dad about it because I'm sure that he wants to surprise me. I wonder if he's going to buy me a Suzuki, or a Yamaha, or a Honda. I wonder if he's going to get me a 125, or a bigger 250, which I could "grow into."

I eagerly do every chore Dad asks me to do, from trimming the hedges to sweeping the driveway to carrying dozens of heavy boxes of old *National Geographic* magazines from the basement to the attic, and then back again when Dad changes his mind. I know he's testing me, to see if I am truly worthy of a new dirt bike, and I am not going to falter. I wonder what colour my new motorcycle will be, and if he'll get me a full-out motocross racer, or an off-road/on-road enduro model.

Finally, after about a couple of weeks of raking, shovelling, carrying, and cleaning, the big moment arrives.

"C'mere, Dak," Dad calls out from inside the garage, "there's something I want to show you."

I drop the rake I've been working with and race across the yard with Smiley bouncing along behind me.

"What is it, Dad?"

"Well, Dak, you're getting older now, and it's time you had some additional things to be responsible for. You've been taking good care of your dog, and you've been doing your chores like a real soldier."

I nod along, knowing from the introduction that this is going to be a bike that will shame even Devin Orff's enormous RM 250.

"Follow me, m'boy," Dad says, and he leads me around behind the garage. With lots of ceremony, Dad pulls the tarpaulin off what I thought was a little stack of firewood, and there it is.

My jaw drops.

In front of me, at just above knee level, stands a battered old mini-bike about the right size for a six-year-old. It is a "Moto-Pup 33" — the "33" meaning that it has a thirty-three cc engine, which is less than one-seventh the size of the engine on Devin Orff's monstrous machine, much smaller than even his least worthy toadie's bike. It looks like a chainsaw with a girls' bicycle seat and two shopping cart wheels. Riding it around in The Badlands will be like trying to fight a squadron of F-16s with a Sopwith Pup biplane. The Bad Boys will run right over me, and over me, and over me again, until my bones and my tiny mini-bike are smashed into particles and ground into the earth.

"So, Sport," Dad beams, "what do you think?"

"Wow, Dad, thanks!" I cry out, not wanting to hurt his feelings. "It's . . . unbelievable!"

"Well, then," he says, "put on the helmet and let's see you take 'er for a spin!"

The helmet. Oh, the helmet. It is covered in a leopard skin print with cartoony green animal eyes painted above the front visor, but the worst part is this: on either side of the helmet, in iridescent purple lettering, are the words ANIMAL WARRIOR. The Bad Boys will not just chase me out of The Badlands; they will kill me and put my skull on a stick as a warning to others who invade their turf.

"Come on, Dak," he urges me, "go try it out!"

So I strap on the ridiculous helmet and sit down on the tiny bike that is so undersized my knees are practically in my armpits. I boot away at the surprisingly tight kick-starter, but the engine will not start. Dad tries to remain patient as he explains that the starter switch has to be in the "on" position before the engine will start, and sure enough, the little motor buzzes to life on the next kick. After stalling the engine a few times, I get the hang of easing the clutch out, and the little bike starts moving, buzzing along like an adrenalized snail.

I discover that the brakes aren't too good as I round the top of the first hill into The Badlands, and sail down the hill at some speed, gravity being more responsible for the mini-bike's velocity than its motor. For the first time since leaving our yard, Smiley had to break from a trot to a run to keep up with me. Since the little engine has so far struggled to pull itself over even the smallest hill, I avoid the steep ones that the Bad Boys had jumped their bikes over with such reckless abandon. Still, it's fun to be moving like this, and Smiley seems to be having a good time running along beside me. I start to laugh, and a bug flies into my mouth and buzzes against my larynx.

I stop to spit out the bug juice, when a noise makes me jump. Over the purring of my engine, I can hear the shriek of a bigger dirt bike racing toward me from the other side of the hill. The bike's back tire just clears the top of my head as it sails over the hilltop. The bike bounces a couple of times as its tires hit the earth, then the rider loses his balance and somersaults across the ground, the bike cartwheeling and crashing on its side.

I put the kickstand of my mini-bike down and run over to where the rider lies.

"Are you okay?"

He sits up and pulls off his helmet, shaking the hair out of his face and cursing a blue streak, totally ignoring me. It is Devin Orff.

Smiley wanders over to Devin and begins licking his face.

"Fuck off fuckin' mutt!"

Smiley just barely dodges the punch Devin throws at him, and beats a hasty retreat back by my side.

Several other dirt bikes roar around the hill and grind to a halt in the dirt around us. The tallest guy gets off his bike and stands over Devin's prone figure. He whips off his helmet and says, "You lose, Orff."

Devin Orff struggles to his feet, trying not to show any pain, and snarls, "No, *you* lose, dickhead. You owe me fifty bucks!"

"Bullshit, Orff," the other kid brays. "You crashed. You owe *me* fifty bucks!"

"I still jumped the hill, fuckface," Devin counters, dragging his left leg slightly as he moves within inches of his nemesis. "You bet me I couldn't jump the hill. I jumped the damn hill, so fucking pay up."

"Fuck off!" says the other kid, "I bet that you couldn't *land* the jump, and you *didn't*. You wiped out!"

One by one, the other riders remove their helmets. I recognize one of them as Cliff Boswink who has held a grudge against me since grade seven when he got suspended from school for giving me a bloody nose. He has never bothered me at school since then, but at this particular moment, we are far, far from school.

"Hey!" Cliff cries out, pointing at me as I attempt to tiptoe back towards my mini-bike. "Why don't you ask *him* if Devin made the jump or not!"

Devin Orff limps toward me, like Frankenstein's Monster. Great.

"You saw me land the jump, didn't you, *buddy*?"

"Um, well ... "

The other guy strides over beside Devin, and joins him in staring at me.

"You saw him crash, didn't you, kid?"

"Well, actually, I — "

"Ha! He saw you crash, Orff, you suckass!" the other kid taunts. "You owe me fifty buckaroos!"

Devin Orff's already reddened face flushes a deeper crimson and he grabs my helmet between his meaty hands and jerks it from my head, the chin strap painfully catching on my ears.

"Nice helmet, dickboy," he says as he tosses my helmet to one of his toadies. "Now listen here, mister *Animal Warrior*. Tell this fucking asswipe that I landed the jump!"

The toadie who has my helmet is scratching on it with a rock. The rest are focused on the conflict between their fearless leader and his potential usurper.

I stutter, "I'm, um, I'm not, um, I'm not sure I saw, um, exactly, um — "

"TELL HIM!" Devin Orff rages, grabbing me by the shoulders and shaking me.

At that moment, another dirt bike comes peeling around the hill with Devin Orff's two Dobermans running along on either side. The rider lifts his helmet's visor to reveal a smaller version of Devin's angry face.

"Devin!" the kid says, "Ma says to git yer ass home for dinner!"

"Tell her to fuck off," Devin replies, letting go of me. "I'll get there when I get there. And you fuck off, too, Billy!"

"Yer gonna get a lickin' when you get home," Billy Orff shouts. He gives his older brother the finger, then roars away in the direction from which he came. The two Dobermans remain, though, and circle over to where Devin stands in front of me, snarling. Instinctively, Smiley snarls back, but not too much. The guy who has been arguing with Devin begins to back away. Devin points a finger at him.

"Chopper! Slash!" he says evenly.

The two dogs begin to snarl, their muscles trembling, straining forward like they are pushing against an invisible wall.

"Fuck!" the kid whimpers, stepping quickly backward. "Don't, Devin! Come on now! Don't!"

"Chopper! Slash! *Sic'im*, boys!" Devin hollers.

The two dogs blast off toward the other boy. He turns to run, but they leap and knock him down from behind. The dogs hold him face down on the ground, growling like demons, their teeth chopping at his arms and legs, and the kid screams in terror, "Fuck! No! Fuck! Orff! Stop 'em! Fuck! Fuck! You win! You win!"

Devin snaps his fingers and says, "Chopper! Slash! *Heel!*"

The dogs back reluctantly away from their victim, still snarling.

"Get the fuck out of here, ya fairy," Devin says to the kid, who is pale and shaking. "Don't come back here without my fifty bucks."

As the other boy starts his bike's engine and rides away, Devin turns his attention to me. His toadies circle like vultures, with that prick Cliff Boswink standing right beside Devin. The one who has been holding my helmet steps up beside Devin.

"Nice bike — a *Moto-Pup!*" Cliff Boswink sneers, scarcely able to contain his glee. "Didj'a get it at a toy store?"

Cliff grabs my helmet from the toadie who held it, then hands it over to Devin. Devin holds it up for all to see, and they all start cackling. The toadie has scratched the letters I and M off, and the stupid lettering on my helmet now reads AN AL WARRIOR. All the Bad Boys roar with laughter.

"Awwww, c'mon boys!" Cliff laughs, "you're gonna make the Anal Warrior *cry*! He might *tell the teacher* on you if you make him cry!"

I turn, get onto my mini-bike, and kick away at the starter, forgetting once again to switch the starter to the "on" position, which makes the Bad Boys laugh even harder.

"Hey, *Anal Warrior!*" Devin calls out, "don't forget your *Anal Warrior* helmet!"

He throws it at me, and it hits me in the side of the face. I reach down to pick it up, lose my balance, and dump my pathetic little mini-bike over. Some of the toadies actually fall on the ground laughing over this. I pick up my little two-wheeled snail, mount it, and buzz away with my knees tucked under my armpits.

A few days later, Dad steps into my room, where, other than to eat lunch and to take Smiley out to pee, I have been sequestered all day reading *Lord of the Rings*.

"Hey, Dak," Dad says. "Aren't you going to get out there and rip around on your mini-bike in the vacant lots? It's a beautiful afternoon for it."

"I'm not feeling very good, Dad."

"Sounds like there's lots of other kids out there having fun on their motorbikes."

Good for them, I thought, *they're probably laughing and waiting for the Anal Warrior to return for another round of humiliation.*

"You do *like* the mini-bike, don't you? You know, your mom still isn't speaking to me . . . "

I just shrug. Dad has my helmet in his hands, which he tosses beside me on the bed.

"I noticed that the letters on it got a bit scuffed up, so I painted the whole thing black for you. I hope you still like it."

"Yeah, it's better, actually."

"Well, good. Get back out there and have some fun."

I don't want to disappoint him, so I say, "Sure, Dad. I'm just going to finish this chapter." I figure I'll listen out the window until the sound of the other engines is gone, then I'll go out for a quick ride.

Dad turns to leave but, when he gets to the doorway, he looks over his shoulder and says, "Life is too short to let anyone stop you from doing what you want to do."

There is maybe an hour of sun left when the hum of engines finally disappears from The Badlands; it is finally safe for me to saddle up the Moto-Pup for a ride. I am doing laps around a hill, with Smiley trotting along happily beside me, when I see one of the most beautiful sights I have ever seen. Above the western horizon, five fingers of deep orange sunlight break through a small cloud, leaving five glowing fingerprints on the surface of the earth. I take a run at the hill with the Moto-Pup, and with a little help from my feet, I manage to coax it up to the top of the hill for a better view.

I kill the engine, remove my helmet, and stretch my arm out towards the sky. When I spread my fingers wide, and bend my wrist downward, it looks as though the sunbeams are flowing directly from my fingertips. I imagine I am a powerful wizard, and the beams of light are actually rays of magic.

Then Smiley begins to growl.

There, in the long shadow of the hill, leaning on their parked bikes, are Devin Orff and Cliff Boswink sharing a cigarette. It is probably hand-rolled and doesn't smell like tobacco. Devin's Dobermans are crouched beside him, their snarls growing louder.

"Look, Devin, it's the Anal Warrior!" Cliff Boswink calls out.

"What the hell ya doin', Anal?" Devin adds. "Prayin' to the queen of the fairies?"

"Nah, Anal's not gay, Orff," Cliff wheezes, "at least not *completely* gay — he's got the hots for some skinny little chick in his class. Zoe's her name. She's *sweeeeeet*."

"Has she got tits yet?" Devin Orff giggles. "Should we go find her and feel her up?"

This imagery is just too much for my brain to handle, and my voice explodes from inside me. "Shut up, jerk!" I yell out. I kick at the starter of the Moto-Pup. I am going to race down the hill at full speed and ram the handlebars right into Devin Orff's crotch for that remark. I kick and kick at the starter but the motor fails to fire.

"*Oooooh*, Anal just called me a *jerk*, Blaster. Maybe we should go have a talk with him about that."

Smiley growls louder as Devin Orff, Cliff Boswink and the two Dobermans saunter up the hill.

Then I remember to turn the starter switch on, and the engine fires on the first kick, but Devin Orff is already standing in front of me, gripping the handlebars of my mini-bike.

"Hey, Anal, don't worry!" he titters. "I'm not gonna hurt you — I just wanna take this hot bike of yours for a ride! Promise I won't break it!"

Even over the buzz of the little engine, I can hear his dogs snarling like demons. Close beside me, Smiley's fur bristles, and he growls back at them.

"Yeah, Anal," Cliff giggles. "We *promise* we won't smash the Moto-Pup into little tiny bits!"

It isn't as big or expensive as their dirt bikes, but the Moto-Pup is a present from my dad, and I am not going to let these two giggling idiots wreck it. I kick the gearshift pedal, wind back the throttle, and drop the clutch, making the doughnut-sized rear tire actually spin a little. It is enough to push Devin Orff out of the way, but there is not nearly enough power to drive through him like I had planned. Now all I can think of is escape, and I buzz down the hill away from Orff and Boswink as fast as the Moto-Pup will carry me, which is slightly faster than they can run on foot.

"Come back here, Anal!" Cliff yells.

They both run after me, but the Moto-Pup gradually pulls ahead enough that they break off their pursuit.

"The name's Dak, shithead!" I yell back as my little bike carries me away. Smiley runs beside me, his mouth wide open and his tongue wagging like a flag, like he's laughing his head off.

"Ha-HAAA, suckers!" I shout over my shoulder.

And then I see them. Devin's attack dogs are charging behind us, gaining quickly. I wrench the throttle back, but it is already open as wide as it will go.

My left foot is jerked from the footpeg. One of the dogs had my pant leg in his teeth! The other Doberman is running beside my right leg, nipping at it. They are going to pull me right off the mini-bike!

A hollow thump! A cyclone of snarling and barking! The dog on the right lets go of my pant leg, and then the second disappears, too. I stand on the rear brake pedal, spin the bike around 180 degrees in the dirt to see Smiley on the back of the dog who had my pant leg in his teeth. The Doberman bucks and thrashes and howls wildly but cannot shake Smiley loose. The second Doberman leaps into the fray, hissing and shrieking like something from hell. The three dogs kick up a cloud of dust, thrashing and snapping and gnashing and snarling wildly.

My hands claw at my face. No no no no no! I would have rather let Devin and Cliff smash up the Moto-Pup and beat me up than watch my dog get killed like this.

But then one of the Dobermans rears up, flips several times in the dust, then sprints away, yelping like an alarm siren. Seconds later, the second Doberman flees like the first, dragging its ass away as fast as its front legs will carry it.

Devin and Cliff, who had been running towards the scene to watch my dog get eaten by the Dobermans, turn tail and run in the opposite direction when Smiley bares his teeth and gallops towards them, barking like crazy. As soon as they are far enough away, Smiley stops his pursuit and trots back to me.

Smiley has a few small cuts on his nose and ears, and he's limping slightly on one paw, but overall he is in pretty good shape for a friendly little mutt that has just taken on two attack dogs at once and kicked the crap out of them. I guess Chopper and Slash's barks are worse than their bites, and it occurs to me that this might be true for their owner and his gang as well.

From this point on, with Smiley running alongside me, I will buzz around The Badlands with a little less fear and a little more joy in my heart.

Pushin' Pickle
(Grade eight)

So, Dak," my father says, in a businesslike tone which always means bad news for me, "how would you like to make some extra money this summer?"

Is this a trick question or something?

"Sure," I answer cautiously.

"Well, great!" Dad cheers, "because I was just talking to Mr. Potzo, and he's going to pull a few strings and get you on at the factory for the summer."

It appears that making a man out of me has become too much work for just one person, so Dad has recruited the neighbourhood men to help out. Like Mr. Potzo, supervisor at the Krispy Green Pickle factory.

"You can meet him in the briefing room in building A-3 at seven on Monday morning. What do you think of that? Your first real job!"

All I can do is nod along. While meeting somebody in the briefing room of A-3 sounds kind of cool, like something that would happen in a James Bond movie, I've also read a few books about the Industrial Revolution, and factories are not portrayed as wonderful places to be. Besides, what self-respecting thirteen-year-old would wake up before seven during summer vacation?

Nevertheless, it is now six-thirty on Monday morning, and I am about to pedal my bike across town to the Krispy Green Pickle factory to meet my fate as a man.

Mom makes me pose for several photos while wearing Dad's workboots and holding my new lunch box.

"Enjoy your first day, honey!" she squeals. It's as if I'm getting on the school bus for my first day of kindergarten.

"Good luck, son," Dad says gravely, as if he is watching a prison bus take me away. "See you at the end of your shift."

The briefing room in A-3 does indeed look like one of those subterranean spy training facilities in James Bond movies: large and windowless, with cinder block walls. There are, however, no Ninja fighters sparring, nor any weapons being tested by men in lab coats, only a couple dozen guys lounging around on plastic chairs. Nobody is blowing the heads off mannequins with missiles launched from fountain pens, either. The only pen in the room is the ballpoint in Mr. Potzo's right hand as he stands at the front of the room making checkmarks on a clipboard.

"Hi, Mr. Potzo!" I say, but he pretends he doesn't know me.

The men in the room are all approaching or past middle age, with beer bellies in varying states of development, and thick, vein-rippled arms. A few of them have military-style brush cuts, and a few have handlebar moustaches or stubbly beards, but every last one of them is wearing the same earth brown work pants. With my old blue jeans, my skinny arms and complete lack of a paunch, I couldn't feel more out of place. I resist the urge to run back to my bike and pedal home at full speed. I am going to make my dad proud of me, even if these guys marinate me in pickle brine and eat me for lunch.

Mr. Potzo glances up from his clipboard at the biggest man in the place. His arms are as big as my torso, encircled with tattoos of pythons and barbed wire. With his shaved head and black goatee, he looks as hard as a coffin nail.

"Bart," says Mr. Potzo, "before you start, take the kid down to L-17 and show him what to do at Station 8."

"Come on, kid," Bart says as he walks over to me. "Gotta getcha to over there before the line starts."

I do as I'm told. I follow silently behind Bart as we wind our way through an obstacle course of huge machines, tanks, and conveyor belts whose main purpose seems to be to generate metallic noise. The inside of the cavernous factory sounds like the noise our lawn mower made, amplified about a hundred times.

"Yer pretty small, kid," Bart grumbles. "You sure yer old enough to be working here?"

"How old do you have to be?" I wonder.

"Sixteen. You *are* sixteen, right?"

"Ah, sure," I lie. If anybody has fibbed on my behalf, I don't want to get them in trouble. No wonder Mr. Potzo ignored me back in the briefing room! "I was born prematurely, that's all."

Bart rolls his eyes and says, "Whatever, kid."

He leads me past a conveyor belt filled with empty pickle jars, beside which an amazingly obese, flush-faced fellow casually leans, using a broom handle as a crutch.

There are sweat stains between the rings of flab that encircle his waist. This guy is so bloated he needs suspenders to hold his brown pants up.

"Hey, Michelin Man!" Bart hollers, in a gruff but friendly way. "Get to work, ya bum! Quit spankin' yer sausage and get sweepin' with that thing!"

"What? With my sausage?" the guy counters with a grin. "Or do you mean the broom?"

I grin. To my thirteen-year-old brain, there is something both funny and liberating about hearing two grown men joking so freely about masturbation, especially when one really does look like the Michelin Man, and the other resembles a WWF wrestling character.

After we have walked farther into the factory, Bart says, "Geeze, kid! Don't you talk?"

"It's loud in here," I offer.

"Hah! Everything's on standby right now while the shifts change — wait until they get the belts going. *Then* you're in for some noise!"

We pass another guy who is lounging in the driver's seat of a forklift truck, his feet resting on the steering wheel's spokes. He is studying a magazine called *Chix*.

"Hey, ya ol' forker!" Bart calls out to him. "Quit pullin' yer goalie and get to work, ya perv!"

Without looking up from his magazine, the forklift truck guy flashes a one-fingered salute in our direction.

"At least I'm not a perv with little boys, Barto," he grunts.

I swallow hard. Where exactly is this Bart guy *really* taking me?

"Don't worry, kid," Bart reassures me. "He's just jokin'. Besides, you ain't my type. Too skinny!"

Changing the subject, I ask, "How come everyone here's got brown work pants? Is there a dress code or something? Nobody told me."

Bart laughs.

"Well, you gotta work here for 90 days before you can be in the union. Once you're in, the company gives ya a pair of brown work pants every month 'cause it ain't fair for guys to have to spend their own money on pants which the pickle brine's just gonna eat away. So when you finally get in the union, they call it getting yer pants. Are you tryin' to get yer pants, or are ya just a summer slave?"

"Uh, summer slave, I guess."

"Oh. Well, once you get yer pants, they've gotta give the best jobs to you first, 'cause you've paid yer dues. Whenever something shitty has to be done, you get a guy who hasn't got his pants yet to do it 'cause he's not in the union yet, and he won't want to stir up any shit with some foreman like Cocksucker Cobb, who'll see that he gets laid off on his 89th day. That sunnuvabitch did that to me three seasons in a row before I finally got my pants!"

Cocksucker Cobb? Could he possibly mean Mr. Cobb, the guy who lives across the street from us and is always yelling at his wife? That guy is in a position of *authority* around here?

"What colour pants does this Cobb guy wear?" I wonder aloud.

"Grey. He's a foreman. Don't let that prick push you around, though."

After another couple minutes of walking around machinery and conveyor belts, I ask, "Are we ever going to get to this L-17 place?"

"We just passed L-14, so L-17's just three away."

"Ah," I nod, but my expression must reveal my confusion.

"L stands for line, bud. Production lines. Each line of machines makes a different kind of pickle. At the far end of the plant, the cucumbers are dumped onto big conveyor belts and sorted into different sizes, then they get carried by other belts to washing machines, then the medium ones go to the slicing machines to make restaurant pickles, the biggest ones go to a grinding machine to make relish, and the small, crisp ones get sent to the lines we're headed for. The cucumbers come in right from the farmers' fields on one end of the building, and they go out the other end as pickles and relish. Cool, eh?"

I can think of lots of other things that are cooler, but I nod anyway. Bart continues talking as we work our way deeper into the factory.

"L-15 to L-21 are used for dill pickles — baby dills, deli-style dills, dills with garlic, dills with garlic and onions — and then there are the special lines, 22 and 23, which are used for makin' Kosher dills. A Rabbi actually comes in, robes 'n' all, to inspect and bless those two lines so Jewish people are allowed to eat 'em. Cocksucker Cobb's in charge of those two lines too — he calls 'em the *kike* lines. What a dick, eh?"

At first glance, Bart looked like this mean dude who would rather step on your face than speak to you. But it turns out that he's this major talker — he should have been a factory tour guide. He knows so much about the machines and personalities inside this factory, it's as if he was born and raised here.

"Well, here we are, sport," he barks, stopping and slapping me on the back, "L-17, Station 8."

Indeed, there is a red plastic plate affixed above a section of narrow, waist-high conveyor belt, which reads "L-17, Station 8." Without Bart as a guide, I wouldn't have been able to find this spot with a map and a compass.

"So, kid, do ya know what pushin' pickle is all about?"

Since here in the Krispy Green Pickle factory world, pulling the goalie, chokin' the Bishop, and spankin' the sausage technically mean masturbating, but seem to also mean slacking off on the job, I can only assume that pushin' pickle means something similar. Not wanting to look like an amateur in front of Bart, I enthusiastically declare that yes, I know what pushin' pickle is all about!

He looks a bit surprised.

"What? Somebody already toldja? Well, what the hell did Potzo send me over here for then? Probably tryin' to make me late for my shift so I'll lose my pants. He's probably in cahoots with Cocksucker Cobb!"

He stomps away, shaking his head.

So here I stand, positioned in front of the narrow conveyor belt, having not even the slightest notion as to what my job is supposed to be. The conveyor belt starts moving, and the noise level multiplies tenfold. From behind a flap on the monstrous machine that towers over me to my left, a train of cucumber-filled jars comes rattling towards me on the conveyor belt. I look around, trying to find clues as to what I'm supposed to be doing.

I notice a big red button next to my post, with the words Emergency Stop stencilled above it. Maybe if there is an emergency, it's my job to push the red button and stop the line. So, I stand there with my finger on the red button, alert and ready.

My big moment finally arrives after twenty minutes, which seems more like three days, when I hear a voice screaming over the din of the machinery, "Stop the line! Stop the fuckin' line!"

An emergency! I jam the red button as hard as I can, nearly spraining my finger in the process. But, I have done my job.

Then I feel the hot wind of someone's breath on the back of my neck.

"Turn around, you shithead! I want to go face-to-face with the motherfucker who — "

I turn around. Inches from my face is the rage-reddened mug of Mr. Cobb, his jowls shaking furiously.

"You stupid fuckup! Do you know what you've done?"

"I stopped the line."

"Do you know what the fuck you're supposed to be doing here? Do ya?"

"Not really, I guess."

"Whadda ya mean, *not really*, ya goddamn *faggot*!"

"Nobody told me what I'm supposed to do."

"Bullshit!" he hollers, and launches a big glob of spit. It lands on the end of my nose. "Who the fuck did Potzo send with you to show you the ropes?"

I don't want to get Bart in trouble, so I simply shrug.

"Then how the fuck did you find your way in here, shithead?"

"With a map and compass," I say, immediately regretting it.

He grabs me by the ear and tugs me further up the line.

"See this, asshole?"

He points to a long conveyor belt jammed with pickle-filled jars.

"The fucking jar-capping machine can't screw the lids on top when there are fucking pickles sticking out the top of the jar! And how the fuck do you think the pickles are supposed to get pushed down into the jars, moron? Huh?"

"Um, with the pickle-pushing machine?" I suggest, realizing as soon as I say it that I'm the pickle-pushing machine.

"*You're* the fucking pickle-pushing machine!" Mr. Cobb confirms, still gripping my ear between his chubby thumb and forefinger. He tugs me over to the belt, which is jammed with jars, and pushes my head down so that my nose is almost inside one of the still-warm jars.

"Now, dickhead, this is what your gonna do, 'cause you're holding up the whole goddamn line. You're gonna take every fucking last one of those jars off the line and put 'em on the floor. Then you're gonna get your ass over there to your station, turn the line back on, and start pushin' them pickles like you ain't never pushed. And on your fuckin' lunch break, you can carry all those jars back over to your station, and push those fuckin' pickles in and run 'em through. Get it?"

Despite the pain it causes my captive earlobe, I nod yes.

"Get goin'! And if so much as one jar breaks on the floor, I am going to kick you in the ass. If a second one breaks, I kick you in the balls. If you break a third one, I'm gonna — "

"What'll ya do if *I* drop a few on the floor, Cobb?" comes a booming voice from behind us. Cobb lets go of my ear. It's Bart.

"Mind your own fucking business," Cobb says.

"If you wanna feel tough, Cobb, why don'tcha try pushin' me around, instead of a kid on his first day."

"If I wanna feel tough, maybe I'll fire your ass, *Bartholomew*," Mr. Cobb says, as he stomps away in the opposite direction.

"Don't worry about it, kid," Bart says. "I'll help you get those jars through during lunch break."

Bart switches the line back on and shows me how the job is done.

"As each jar passes, you grab the jar between your knuckles, and push any pickles which are stickin' outta the jar *into* the jar with yer thumbs."

"That's it?"

"It's the toughest damn job in the whole factory, bud," he says. "Why do you think nobody with their union pants is doin' it?"

Bart steps back, and I take over. I grab the first jar between my knuckles and ram a protruding pickle into the jar with my thumbs. Then another. Then another. Another. Another. Man, do these jars move fast!

"How do you think I got all these muscles?" Bart says as he walks away. "Three seasons of pushin' pickle."

By the time the horn blows for lunch break, my thumbs are completely paralyzed and I am unable to fold them back in. My wrists are throbbing and swollen. My elbows have begun to ache and, through the magic of muscle burn, I've discovered my underused triceps and shoulder muscles. With my wrists turned up and my thumbs frozen in position, I must look like a geeky, skinny version of The Fonz.

As promised, Bart shows up to help me with the job. With his help, it's done in a few minutes. He carries my lunch box to the cafeteria for me since I can't convince my hand to close around the handle. When some of the other guys in the cafeteria see me holding my sandwich sideways between my immobilized palms, turning my head sideways for each bite, they look at each other and say, "pushin' pickle."

I'm not even half-finished with my sandwich when Cobb shows up at the cafeteria entrance.

"Sifter!" he barks, "get over here!"

Cobb is leaning on a long stick, like the handle of a rake.

I stand up straight, straining against the aches in my upper body, and walk over to him. Cobb's knobby nose hovers just beneath my chin.

"Just wanted to inform you that the company requires that employees wear steel-toed safety boots," he says, in an even tone of voice. "Are your boots steel-toed?"

"I don't know. They belong to my dad."

"Your *dad*? The overpaid, got-the-whole-fuckin'-summer-off *English teacher*? Your dad the *pussy* owns *workboots*?"

This pisses me off and I shoot off my mouth.

"Are those *steel-toed* running shoes you're wearing, Mr. Cobb?"

His thick neck begins to redden at the collar.

"I'm the boss, dipshit. I can wear whatever the fuck I want."

The cafeteria has fallen silent. Cobb jabs the end of the poking stick into the toes of my right foot and leans his substantial weight onto it.

"Ow!" I yelp.

"Guess they're not steel-toed, eh? An *English teacher* wouldn't have steel-toed boots. Your pussy dad can't even teach you to mow the fucking lawn!"

"At least my dad isn't teaching me to abuse my mother," I say under my breath.

"What did you say, pussy boy?"

"I said I'll get some steel-toed boots for tomorrow, sir."

For the rest of the afternoon, I manage to keep up with the speed of the line. My clothes are saturated with sweat, and my entire body feels like it's made of jelly, but I fight on. This is a battle I cannot lose. Of course, in the time it takes this manly thought to cross my synapses, my left arm seizes up. I can't move it at all. Frantically, I pound the pickles into the jars with my functioning right fist, but it occurs to me that I will soon break my hand if I keep it up. Angry at myself, I slam the red button.

Cobb immediately comes running.

"Turn that line back on! There are ten minutes left in the shift!"

Just ten minutes? Boy, time flies when you're miserable and frantic.

A few of the other men begin to walk past us, toward the time clock, thinking the shift is over. Cobb chases after them.

"Hey! Hey! There's still ten minutes left! Get back here!"

The men keep walking.

"Goddammit, get back here!"

Cobb loses his temper. He kicks one of the machines, and his cursing momentarily stops. He falls to the concrete holding his foot, rolling back and forth, howling like he's just been shot with a .44 Magnum.

"My toe! My toe! Christ, I broke my fuckin' toe!"

The shift change horn blows, and all of the workers from the surrounding lines come over to see what's going on. The men who had departed early from L-17 also wander back. This is a show that nobody wants to miss.

And now I commit a serious error of judgment. I wander over to where Cobb is rolling around and say:

"Gee, Mr. Cobb, guess you should have been wearing those steel-toed boots, eh?"

Cobb's face turns from red to purple as the other workers laugh at him. He shimmies across the floor on his butt, still cradling his injured foot in one hand, and reaches up onto the halted conveyor belt. With his free hand, Cobb grabs a jar of pickles. Jowls shaking, his face glowing crimson, he screams:

"God! Damn! Fucking! Smartass! Kid!"

He hurls the jar at me with all his strength. I raise my stiff arms to shield my face. The jar shatters against my wrists.

I slowly lower my arms from my face, and the shard of glass buried deep in my left wrist comes into focus. I watch with fishbowl-eyes as my blood begins to spurt from the gash, spattering on the concrete, speckling my shirt, my jeans, and my dad's workboots. Pain sizzles where the vinegar from the pickle brine has penetrated the wound.

My memory of the rest of the day is sketchy. There are a few images of a nurse cleaning my wound, a doctor stitching the gash back together, the feeling of plaster hardening around my forearm and wrist. Through the blur of strong painkillers, I vaguely remember Mom and Dad helping me into the car just outside the emergency room exit.

I'm still not sure if I dreamed this next part, but I'm pretty sure it was real. After Dad wheeled the car into our driveway, he squinted into the rear-view mirror, and with his lips tight and his jaw muscles bulging, he jumped from the car without even closing the door. With the engine running, he strode across the street to where Mr. Cobb was sitting on his porch with his injured foot propped up on a pillow.

I couldn't hear their conversation, but it was short. Dad's voice was a lot louder than Mr. Cobb's, and Dad *definitely* had the last word. His face was white when he reached into the car to turn off the ignition. He did not slam the car door when he closed it, and his voice had its usual even timbre as he and Mom helped me into the house.

"Mr. Cobb has been made to understand that he will be in danger of suffering more than a sore foot if he bothers you again. If he forgets about this agreement, you will be sure to tell me about it, okay?"

"Okay, Dad."

A few hours later, my brain is pleasantly humming from the effects of the painkillers. Dad shuffles in to my room to check on me.

"How's it going, there, Bud?" he says from the doorway of my room.

"My wrist hurts."

Dad comes a little closer to my bed.

"Well, Dak, I'm proud of you," he says. "You really took it like a man."

Then Dad straightens up and clears his throat, the way he always does when the sentimentality-resistance circuit in his brain kicks in.

He pretends he doesn't hear me when I say, "So did you, Dad."

KRISPY GREEN PICKLE, Inc.
is pleased to announce the

Retirement

of
CHESTER L. COBB,
Factory Foreman

An informal gathering for Mr. Cobb will be held in
The Jeremiah Faire Room of the Faireville Mental
Health Centre this Saturday to thank him for his
many years of service.
No gifts please!

Benjamin's Aliens

(Grade nine, with grade three flashbacks)

When we were eight, Benjamin Cranston was obsessed with finding a way to escape planet earth. Now, six years later, it seems that he has finally achieved his goal.

Even though we lived on opposite sides of the city, I suppose that I was destined for a while to become Benjamin's best friend. I really didn't have much choice; a force greater than either Benjamin or myself was involved in bringing us together: The Faireville District Board of Education.

When my parents read me the letter that the school board sent them, I assumed that a "pilot project" had something to do with learning to fly an airplane. Naturally, I agreed to participate as any right-thinking, career-minded eight-year-old would have done. Instead of getting the flight training I expected, I was removed one afternoon from my grade three classroom and subjected to what my tormentors referred to as a battery of cognitive abilities tests. If you have ever been subjected to such testing, you will probably agree that the use of the word battery (as in assault and battery) is fairly accurate.

Before the end of the following week, I was attending a special school, which was so new that it hadn't even been given its own building yet, or even its own official name. Everyone involved simply referred to it as the Gifted School. It was located, for the time being, in a large, echoey room in the basement of an ancient, half-deserted technical high school on the other side of the city.

It was in this cavernous room that I first met Benjamin. I could only guess that he had made the same mistake as I: the accidental demonstration of abnormal ways of understanding certain things. Benjamin's crimes against being average were far more outstanding than my own; while I was certainly guilty of an early predisposition towards literacy, Benjamin was able to understand physics, chemistry, and engineering principles in the same way that other children understand Hot Wheels cars and Barbie dolls.

Benjamin and I were the only real children in the entire program, so we didn't have much choice but to spend a lot of time together. A dozen teenagers were also sequestered in that big, drafty room but just like the harried instructor in charge of our education, these older kids usually ignored us. As a result, Benjamin and I were given free rein to do a lot of "hands-on, student-directed learning," which was edubabble for "fooling around mostly unsupervised."

During our stay, we produced an inspiring assortment of toys, machines, models, and best of all, real chemical reactions (which were often stinky, smoky, explosive, or, in the best case studies, a combination of the three). I learned many things during my stay at the Gifted School: to this day I am still capable of producing a multitude of dangerous chemical reactions with ordinary household substances.

The program, by the way, was cancelled three months later. Perhaps it was because few of us brought home anything for our parents to display on the doors of their refrigerators, but more likely the cancellation was a result of the fire that burned the old Tech School to the ground. The program's end didn't really matter much, because by then, Benjamin and I had become best friends. Boys who make explosions together are friends forever. Blood may be thicker than water but explosives are more powerful than blood.

"I'm glad the fire happened," Benjamin confided to me. "I hated going to that school. But I'm sure glad I met you, Dak."

After we returned to our usual, everyday, readin'-writin'-and-'rithmatic classrooms, we saw each other less frequently — perhaps for one weekend every two months. Getting permission from my parents for even this limited contact required a great deal of whining and brooding since Benjamin's house was some distance from our own, and also since his parents didn't seem to make much of an impression on my own mom and dad.

We usually opted for Benjamin's house, because his parents were more permissive about our experiments and expeditions than mine. In fact, Benjamin's mom and dad were often pleasantly absent for entire afternoons, unlike my own parents, who hovered over us like surveillance helicopters every time Benjamin came to visit. There was, of course, a rather damning correlation between Benjamin's presence and the number of physically altered household implements which surfaced afterwards. I never worried much about the little accidents that occasionally accompanied our projects, though; compared with the greater rewards of scientific exploration, they were small sacrifices indeed.

The first time Benjamin invited me to sleep over at his house, he was busy planning an underground space station. I often made such plans myself, which would usually hang on the refrigerator for a few weeks before migrating into a trash bag to make room for plans of even greater proportion. Benjamin's plans, however, were not just amusements, nor were they simply boyhood fantasies. When Benjamin made a plan, it was meant to be carried out. Benjamin's imagination was much less gaseous than my own.

Benjamin didn't have much choice in the matter; he was convinced that aliens, who lived on the other side of the universe, were communicating with him. The aliens are coming to Earth, and they sent specific telepathic instructions so that things will be in order when they arrive.

"How come they don't communicate with me, Benjamin?" I asked him.

"You're just a normal human, Dak," was his reply. "You may have been chosen for that gifted class, but you haven't got a brain like mine. I'm different. The aliens have told me so. They need me. Their world can't survive without me, and I have to get ready for them to come and take me away from here soon. You can help me build the underground receiving station for when they come, but I'm the only one that can go with them."

At this point, he had already started to march purposefully towards his father's tool shed.

"What are you talking about, Benjamin?" I asked him. This was a question I had become quite accustomed to asking.

He sighed and rolled his eyes the way he always did when he felt he was dealing with a lesser human, one incapable of fully understanding his purposeful schemes.

"They're underground dwellers, see," he would explain. "So we'll have to build a reception station for them beneath the ground. We'll feed them orange juice and nectarines because they subsist mostly on vitamin C. Their matter-transporting device will materialize inside our station and they'll take me away with them so I can save their world. I am the Chosen One. They have told me this. They need me."

I have never been one to interfere with the imaginings of others, so I played along.

"Oh, I see. Can I help?"

"Of course, you can help! Do you think building an underground base is easy work for just one guy?"

With shovels as tall as ourselves and with all the strength we could summon from our skinny little bodies, we proceeded to dig a hole in Benjamin's parents' backyard, a hole which would eventually become his subterranean alien friendship centre, his extraterrestrial welcome wagon. By nightfall, the hole was just big enough for Benjamin and I to lie down in — for some reason, this was important.

"Perfect," said Benjamin. "This is exactly the size they want. Tomorrow we can lay the boards across and put the grass back on top. No stupid adults will ever know the difference. The aliens will come and go. I'll be gone before my parents even notice."

All of that digging made us quite hungry, so we searched through the Cranstons' rather dark bungalow, looking for Benjamin's mother. We found her sitting on the floor behind the basement bar. Tributaries of eyeliner were drying on her cheeks, and I knew that there was something very wrong. I knew that I should have called my parents right then and got them to come and take me home, but I feared that if I did, I would probably never see Benjamin again. Half the books I had read up to this point in my life stressed the importance of loyalty to friends. I kept my mouth shut.

"Hey, Mom, this is Dak, my buddy from the old Gifted School. Will you make us some supper?"

His Mom looked up at us. She seemed to have dark circles under her eyes, like a raccoon, but it was difficult to see clearly in the dim basement light.

"Get something from the fridge, will you honey?" she said. The tone of her voice made me shiver, but again I resisted the urge to run to the phone and call home. I would stick by my friend.

"Okay, Mom," said Benjamin, and we scuttled off towards the stairs.

"What's the matter with your mother?" I asked, rather meekly.

"Oh, nothing, she just likes to sit back there behind the bar, that's all. It's her special place, where she gets away. It's nothing."

His mother called out to us as we scampered through to the kitchen.

"Boys! Try to be quiet, okay? Benjamin's Daddy isn't, um, feeling very well."

There wasn't much worth eating in the fridge, so we raided the pantry instead. We tiptoed up the stairs to the attic where Benjamin liked to sleep — his bedroom was usually too cluttered to be slept in anyway. We spread our supper of potato chips, cola, Twinkies, chocolate pudding, and peanut butter out on the floor in front of us. I was going to bring along some nectarines, but Benjamin reminded me that those were for the aliens.

As Benjamin changed into his pyjamas, I noticed a large, purple-brown bruise in the center of his chest.

"Hey, Benjamin, what happened to you?"

"What? What do you mean? Oh, the bruise. Um, well, one of my inventions malfunctioned, that's all. I was building a spring-loaded rock-cannon, and it acciden-tally went off."

"Wow! You built a rock-cannon? Can I see it?"

Benjamin suddenly became angry, the way he some-times did when one of the other kids in his neighbour-hood showed up to see if he wanted to come out and play. Benjamin had no use for little minds, or for people who couldn't understand the immensity of his life's purpose. Couldn't they see that he had more important things to do, and that he was preparing for a great journey into the unknown?

"No!" he barked at me. "No, you can't see the damn rock-cannon, okay! I told, you, it's malfunctioning! It doesn't work! Are you deaf or something?"

"Geeze, take it easy!" I replied, a little frightened at his outburst, but also a bit perturbed.

"I'm gonna go home if you're gonna start acting like a jerk!"

His behaviour quickly changed.

"No, no — don't go home. Don't leave. I'm sorry. I need you to help me finish the station. It has to be completed or the aliens will have no place to transport to. I'm sorry I yelled at you . . . "

He now sounded as if he might start crying.

"Forget about it," I mumbled. Sometimes Benjamin could be a difficult character to understand.

I didn't sleep very well that night. I kept having strange nightmares, nightmares with no pictures, only sound. I imagined that I was hearing muffled sounds of anguish crying, hollering, things breaking. I dreamt that these things were going on beneath me, maybe two or three floors down. A couple of times, the dreams were so real that I thought I could hear the sounds continuing after I was awake. I was so frightened, I may have even cried a little. I kept telling myself, you're only dreaming, none of this is really happening — hell is not breaking loose downstairs.

"How was your sleep-over, Honey?" Mom asked when I returned home.

"Fun!" I gushed. "We played a lot. Benjamin's got cool toys. And his mom is a really great cook!"

I felt a little guilty lying to my mom like that, but I knew that she would never allow me to visit Benjamin again if I let on that his household was so much different than our own.

I didn't see Benjamin for three months, although I talked to him on the phone quite often. He was making good progress in equipping the interior of his underground station. He had even gone so far as to smuggle a portable electric heater from the house to the station. He had also taken to sleeping outside beneath the ground, since the aliens had informed him that they might decide to come get him during the night. Logically, the aliens thought that it would be less dangerous if their rendezvous with Benjamin occurred during the night.

The next time I visited him, we went to bed early. Although I wasn't particularly keen on the idea, Benjamin insisted that we sleep outside in his underground fort, beneath the boards and sod and grass. He had brought out extra blankets and rations to make my stay as comfortable as possible, but I must admit that lying in the dirt under the ground in somebody else's backyard is not the most restful situation. I was afraid that the whole thing might collapse on us.

Benjamin slept soundly, curled up in a tight ball with his fingers in his mouth. When his alarm clock sounded at 3:00 o'clock, I was still fully awake.

"Come on!" he whispered excitedly. "We've got an important mission to accomplish tonight!"

Even with the flashlight, the tiny space in the ground was still dark. We struggled into our clothes and emerged into the cool, moonlit night. Our surroundings actually seemed bright in comparison with the black void in which we had spent most of the night. With my eyes fully adapted to the darkness, there was no mistaking that Benjamin removed a very large can of gasoline from bushes at the far side of the backyard lawn.

"What are we doing, Benjamin?" I was afraid to hear his answer, but also partly exited.

"The aliens have been having a hard time finding me, Dak," he whispered. "Their scanners have been scrambled by certain particles in our upper atmosphere, and they haven't been able to locate my underground base, yet."

"But what are we going to do with the gas, Benjamin?"

"They're going to try to locate me visually. I'm going to write my name in fire so they can see where I am through their telescopes."

I was no longer enthusiastic about any of this. I was only afraid. I tried to think of a reason to stop him.

"Um, do you think the light from fire will be strong enough to be seen all the way across the galaxy? Probably not, eh?"

It was the best deterrent I could think of under the circumstances.

Benjamin began pouring gasoline on the ground. A wet letter "B" was already starting to soak into the earth before he bothered to answer my question.

"Are you stupid or something, Dak? Their telescopes are at least a thousand times more powerful and a million times more accurate than our junky little Earth telescopes. And just in case you've forgotten, the aliens live on the other side of the universe, not the galaxy. If it were just the galaxy, I'd be long gone by now."

Having spelled out his name in such a way that it covered almost the entire backyard, Benjamin removed a book of dime-store matches from his back pocket and struck one on the outside cover.

"Besides, I have to use fire — the aliens' spectro-graphic analyzers are specifically calibrated to detect the light spectrum of gasoline fire in an oxygen-based atmosphere. So relax!"

He dropped the match at the base of the last letter "N."

"Well, I guess this is it, Dak. By tomorrow night, I'll be a million light-years from this stupid planet."

The match flickered for a moment, then with a surprising roar, the entire word burst into flame, and Benjamin's name illuminated everything around it. For a moment I was lulled — hypnotized by the allure of dancing fire.

Then, panic. Sheer panic. The flames that formed the word "BENJAMIN" began to spread. An appendage of the letter "E" advanced up the trunk of a tree. Another limb of flame swatted at the tool shed. Another licked at the wooden fence and still another crawled along the row of hedges. Within seconds, the entire yard was engulfed in an orange roar. Benjamin's name became indistin-guishable from the rage that flashed all around us.

We ran screaming into the house.

"Mom! Mom! Mom!" Benjamin hollered. It was the first time I had ever seen Benjamin in tears.

His mother emerged from the basement, still slit-eyed from interrupted sleep. The glow from the backyard flickered on her face for a moment before she realized what was happening.

"Oh my God," she muttered, as she slid sideways towards the telephone.

"Oh my God!" she began to scream. "Oh my God!"

Benjamin's father appeared from upstairs.

"What the hell is all the racket . . . ?"

Benjamin began to sob.

"I'm sorry, Daddy, I'm sorry. I'm sorry."

His father walked directly to where Benjamin stood, and looked him straight in the face, unblinking, nostrils flared.

"Did you do this?" his father whispered.

"I'm sorry. I'm sorry. I'm sorry," Benjamin whispered back.

His father raised a huge fist into the air.

Benjamin began to shriek.

"I'm sorry! I'm sorry! Sorry sorry sorry sorry sorry!

With a swift, downward swing, the hovering fist slammed against the side of Benjamin's face, sending him spiralling to the floor.

Screaming those nightmare screams I had heard on an earlier night, Benjamin's mother ran towards him where he lay, quiet and motionless. She never got there because she was met halfway by her husband's fist. There was a loud crack, like the sound of a hammer whacking a board, and Benjamin's mother hit the floor.

Whimpering, she continued to crawl towards her son.

"Stay where you are, woman!" bellowed the father. "You leave that little bastard right where he is!"

The father stomped towards the telephone, cleared his throat, and spoke evenly into the receiver.

"Hello? Faireville Fire Department? Listen, we've got an emergency here at 43 Appletree Crescent. Our backyard is on fire and it may shortly be our house. Yes, thank-you. The sooner, the better."

That was the last I ever saw of Benjamin's house, or either of his parents. I ran out the front door and called my parents from a nearby convenience store.

In the car on the way home, my mother began to cry, saying that she always had a feeling that there was something odd about those people. Dad seemed pretty upset, too. Mom wrapped her arms around me and held me tight, and Dad drove with one hand, his free arm circling us.

An official investigation concluded that the fire was started by "an accidental fuel spill," and that Benjamin and his mother "sustained minor injuries in the ensuing panic." Despite this official clemency, I was forbidden to visit Benjamin's house again. He stopped calling me on the phone, and I didn't invite him to stay at my house anymore.

Six years passed before I saw Benjamin again. By that time, the status and stigma of being a child prodigy had slowly faded from my existence, and I was enjoying the life of a normal fifteen-year-old boy. After my stint at the Gifted School, I carefully refrained from too much intellectual development by devoting most of my thoughts to the mystery of girls. Many of my classmates eventually caught up with me.

In high school, it was easier to blend in, to become part of the great multi-tentacled adolescent mass. In fact, I became accepted by my peers to such an extent that I somehow managed to acquire a girlfriend. She was (and still is) Zoe Perry. I liked her even when we went to

Faireville Elementary School together, but it wasn't until high school that it became okay for me to actually have her as a girlfriend.

Anyway, I'm sure that even if the fire at the Gifted School hadn't happened, and even if I hadn't been streamed back into the regular school system, I probably would have quit hanging around with Benjamin by the time I reached high school. Benjamin and I were friends because we were different than everybody else. By grade 9, I wasn't all that different.

But Benjamin did not simply disappear from my life. His name nonchalantly resurfaced one afternoon when Zoe was over at my house. We were working on a newspaper research project for our Canadian politics course, when an article caught her attention.

"Hey, Dak!" she said, from behind her newspaper. "Take a look at this one! This is wild! *'Boy Injured in Bizarre Accident . . . Fourteen-year-old Benjamin Cranston, of West Faireville, was hospitalized yesterday with multiple fractures and lacerations, as the result of an accident involving the use of a giant working catapult which the teenager had built from scavenged parts.'* Can you believe what some people will do for attention?"

"Give me that!" I said.

It was true. There, embedded in the hues of newspaper grey, was Benjamin: six years older than the last time I had seen him, and partially obscured by bandages. I felt tremendous guilt. I knew I would have to contact him, or else I would never be able to purge the image of that newspaper photograph from my mind.

To avoid a potential confrontation with my parents, who believed in leaving past traumas alone, I sneaked away that evening to visit Benjamin in the hospital. I must admit that I did think twice about it. Some friend, eh?

Benjamin was all smiles when I got there, and he didn't seem the least bit surprised to see me, despite the six-year hiatus. He intentionally kept me at bay for awhile with small talk before actually making any mention of the circumstances which had put him in the hospital. Perhaps this was his way of chastising me for the lapse in our interactions.

Finally, though, he explained everything.

Since his plan to be taken away by aliens was aborted, due to the backyard fire, he and the aliens had devised an alternate plan. They would simply scoop up Benjamin in one of their space ships as they flew by. All Benjamin had to do was build a catapult which would hurl him into the air as the ship flew past.

Of course, I knew that he was joking. He was just referring to something that happened long ago — a fantasy which had been part of our times together. He was simply trying to break the ice in his own unusual way. I decided to play along.

"Why couldn't you just stay on the ground and let the space ship scoop you up, Benjamin?" I laughed.

"Well, see, there's a reason for that. Their propulsion systems create an effect around the ship similar to that of a vacuum. If they come too close to the surface of a planet they are drawn towards it and they crash. When they flew by, they missed me. It was my own fault. I was about a metre short of the minimum flight level for one of their cruisers."

Benjamin began to chuckle again, despite the obvious pain that the movement caused him.

"Well, what now?" I asked, unsure of my real desire to hear his reply.

"I'll tell you this much, Dak. I sure won't make the same mistake again!"

"You mean you're going to forget about the catapult idea?" I asked hopefully.

"Oh, no, of course not. I can't let a few little injuries get in the way of the next giant step for human evolution, can I? I'm just going to have to put a better spring on the catapult, so it will throw me above the minimum flight level of the cruisers, that's all."

He stopped to clear his throat.

"In the meantime, though, until my bones mend and I get my strength back, I'm going to work on an electronic transmission device so the aliens can communicate more easily with me."

I was beginning to grow tired of this silliness.

"But Benjamin, I thought the aliens talked to you through telepathy."

"Oh, they do, they do, but lately I've been having these awful headaches, see. Sometimes they're so bad they make me throw up. The aliens think they could be caused by over-exerting my underdeveloped human telepathic abilities. So, logically, I'm going to build a transmitter."

"Ah. Logically."

Benjamin eventually fell asleep, dreaming about his aliens, no doubt. I returned home feeling no better about anything, and wondering if I really should have seen him at all. My mind offered no explanations, no solutions. I could only shrug.

Two days later, it comes as a very great shock to me when I receive a telephone call from Benjamin's mother.
Benjamin is dead.
For some crazy reason, I ask her if she means that Benjamin is just missing.
No. He is dead. There is a body.
She hangs up, crying.

I have been to a couple of funerals before, but they have always been funerals for the old. Benjamin was my age. The darkness feels a lot closer than it ever did before.
I deduce from the buzz of conversation that surrounds me that, technically speaking, Benjamin died of strangulation; he was hung by one of those crazy inventions of his. To be more specific, a rope was tied to the end of the launcher on Benjamin's catapult and this rope somehow got wrapped — six times — around his neck just as the catapult fired.
The word "suicide" is being cautiously avoided at the funeral. People use the word "accident" instead.
I think about Benjamin's other accidents now and I wish I had understood what was really happening then. Some prodigy I was! First I thought he was just playing. Then I thought he was crazy. Then, when all else failed, I quit thinking about him altogether.
I am not feeling very smart at all. By gritting my teeth hard, I am able to prevent myself from crying out.
Benjamin's mother weeps uncontrollably. His father stands stiffly nearby, looking incredibly stalwart for a

man who has just lost his only son. The other guests engage in small talk, pretending that they don't feel the weight upon them.

The funeral makeup covers Benjamin's bruises pretty well, but even so, I know they are there. They are everywhere. Benjamin's bruises are all over the room. They are on me, too, and I fear that time will not have much luck healing them.

The police found a note taped to the base of Benjamin's catapult. They dismissed it as the scribblings of a lunatic.

It read:

> *No Aliens AT ALL*
> *None*
> *NO Aliens*
> *NONE.*

Searchlight TV
(Grade ten)

'm unable to sleep at night because any possibility of Zoe Perry remaining my girlfriend has disappeared. My younger sister Charlotte, through channels apparently only available to annoying elementary-school girls, found out from her equally annoying little friend Clarisse Tanner, that Zoe has started dating Clarisse's older brother, Jimmy. Charlotte was only too happy to inform me of this development. She loves to see me suffer.

Jimmy Tanner is this puffed-up pretty-boy creep in grade eleven. I'm not sure what Zoe can possibly see in him. Clearly, she must think I'm smarter, because she studies with *me*, not *him*. I'm pretty sure I'm taller than him, too. The only thing I can think of is that Jimmy's parents are rich, and they have given him his own car (a shiny red Camaro) which is very useful for taking girls on dates.

I turned sixteen a couple of weeks back and I've already passed my driver's test so only one last hurdle remains: If I am going to pry Zoe away from Jimmy Tanner before I go crazy with desire for her, I am going to have to get a car. And since my parents are definitely not the Rockefellers, I will need a second job to afford one before Jimmy and Zoe get married, have kids, grow old together, and get buried side-by-side in the family plot.

I've been scanning the Help Wanted section in the *Faireville Examiner*, and there are a few jobs that would pay the kind of money I need. The problem is that they contain discouraging phrases like "experience necessary" or "post-secondary education required." I am about to face the grim prospect of losing the love of my life to a weasel with a red Camaro, when in today's paper I see it, the ad which will help make Zoe Perry mine:

SEARCHLIGHT TV

Faireville's only choice for
Television Sales & Service
is looking for a motivated individual
for
SATURDAY DELIVERIES &
INSTALLATIONS.

Driver's license necessary.

DOUBLE MINIMUM WAGE PAID!

See owner Liam Capper at store for interview.
JESUS BLESS AND
FORGIVE YOU!

JESUS SAVES!

I also see Searchlight TV's weekly full-page ad in the *Faireville Examiner* in which the "t" in Searchlight is shaped like a cross. The store's owner must be on pretty good terms with Jesus to use one of His trademarks in a business logo! Every Searchlight TV ad concludes with the lines, "Jesus forgive you," and "Jesus Saves!" but after comparing their prices with the ads from the city newspaper, it seems to me that if *Jesus* saves at Searchlight TV, everybody else gets ripped off.

Nevertheless, if I want to win Zoe's affections away from Jimmy Tanner, I need to make some extra cash. I immediately walk downtown to Searchlight TV to apply for the job.

The interior of Searchlight TV is dusty and claustrophobic, lit with dim incandescent bulbs hanging on wires from the ceiling. The televisions are haphazardly displayed with the front of each box chopped off to show the appliance inside. Clearly Liam Capper is not making many sales based on the aesthetics of his store yet he can afford full-page ads in the local paper. What is the secret of his success?

At the back of the sales floor, beneath a huge cardboard sign that reads "Jesus forgive you!" a young woman rests her palms on a paper-strewn countertop, contemplating the paint flaking from the ceiling. There is no makeup on her face and her long hair is tied in a braid. She wears a long-sleeved blouse and a floor-length skirt like a pioneer woman. A few feet in front of her, two men and a woman are gathered around a partially opened television box. This woman also has her hair in a long braid and is dressed in a long, bland dress like the girl behind the counter. The two men are arguing over the price of a television set.

"But, Liam," says the taller man, "four ninety-nine still seems like an awfully high price for such a small television."

The shorter man is obviously Liam Capper, the store's owner.

"Ronald," he moans, "you have to understand that we sell only top-quality, premium-brand electronics like Panasonic and Sony — not the junk those discount stores sell!"

A quick look at the stacks of televisions reveals that this is not entirely true. The logos on the TVs *look* like name-brand sets, but they actually say Pan*i*sonic and S*a*ny. The *Assembled in Laos* labels on the boxes are still partially legible under the scribble of black marker.

"But Liam," begs Ronald, "this same TV is selling for *two* ninety-nine in the city!"

Liam Capper spreads his arms wide and wails, "Ronald! You're not telling me you would be willing to put your hard-earned money into the hands of a *sinful, idolatrous* corporate discount store, are you? They can offer lower prices because they cut *Jesus* out of the picture! You know that a portion of the proceeds of every sale at Searchlight TV goes right back to our own beloved church, *don't you?*"

"Well, sure, Liam," says the taller man, "but four ninety-nine still seems like a lot."

Liam Capper's eyes bulge maniacally, an effect that is amplified by the thick lenses of his eccentrically large glasses. He does not fit the image of what I supposed a man of Jesus would look like. He is short with a sunken chest, stumpy legs, and disproportionately large fore-arms. His bristling red hair has receded several inches, making his forehead shine like a pink light bulb. Yet wiry hair grows in abundance everywhere else — sticking out from under his rolled-up sleeves and bursting from his open collar, nearly concealing the enormous gem-encrusted crucifix against his chest. Liam Capper looks like a cross between a high school chess club geek, a '70s pimp, and Popeye the Sailor Man.

"You heard Reverend Rathburn's sermon last week on supporting your fellow parishioners, *didn't you?*" he rails. "Did he not mention a number of local businesses who are endorsed *exclusively* by the Church of the Lord's Holy Command?"

"Well, yes, of course, but — "

"And was Searchlight TV not one of those busi-nesses?"

"Well, sure, but — "

"And are you telling me that you *doubt* the words of our Holy Reverend?" Missiles of spit fly from Liam Capper's lips as his voice reaches a quavering crescendo. "You are *unwilling* to *trust* the man whom *Jesus himself* trusts more than any other?"

"Of course I trust the Reverend, Liam!"

"Very good then," says Liam Capper, dropping the moral indignation routine. "WANDA!" he bellows.

Behind the counter, the young woman snaps to atten-tion. Without a trace of irony, she answers, "Yes, my loving master?"

"Write up a bill of sale for a Panisonic 17-inch TV," he sighs. "And give him our highest congregation-member's discount — four *eighty*-nine." He turns to

Ronald and whispers, "We usually only give this sort of deep discount to the Reverend himself, so keep it under your hat!"

"Oh, I will, I will! *Jesus forgive you*, Liam!"

"*Jesus forgive you*, too, Ronald," Liam says, as he walks into the backroom behind the counter.

Wanda smiles vacantly while a noisy old dot matrix printer cranks out a receipt. She absently switches the floppy disk in the computer, and prints out a second receipt. Ronald signs them and scribbles out a cheque. Wanda continues smiling like a plastic doll as she tears a carbon copy from one of the receipts and hands it to Ronald, who hurries out of the store with his wife, looking like an infidel who has just escaped the Spanish Inquisition.

"*Jesus forgive you!*" Wanda cheerfully calls out as the door creaks shut behind them.

Something about this is very weird, and I have a strong feeling that I should walk out right behind them, but the words DOUBLE MINIMUM WAGE from the Help Wanted ad leap into my head, so I walk to the counter instead.

"Um, hello," I say to Wanda. "I'm here to apply for the delivery job."

"Delivery job?" she hazily asks, looking as if she is trying to decide whether or not I am really here. "Oh yes. Liam fired Corky last week, didn't he?" She fades into herself for a moment.

Perhaps Corky didn't love Jesus enough. I'd have to make sure to come across as extra pious.

Suddenly she says brightly, "Oh! I'll go back and get Liam! He's in his office."

I am left standing alone at the counter for at least twenty minutes before she returns with Liam Capper. While wondering what the two of them could possibly be doing back there for so long, my bored eyes wander across the countertop to the copy of the receipt for Ronald's new TV which Wanda had left lying there. Right beside it, in plain view, is *another* copy of the same bill, but *with different numbers on it*! The original receipt shows that Ronald paid $609 for the TV (including taxes and mysterious fees), yet the second bill shows that Searchlight TV charged only $365! Again my instincts tell me to leave the store but the temptation of DOUBLE MINIMUM WAGE, like the apple to Adam, is impossible to resist.

Liam Capper finally strides in from the rear of the store with Wanda following a few paces behind, her eyes cast down. Liam Capper thrusts his hand in my direction and says, "Sorry to keep you waiting here for so long, but I needed Wanda to, uh . . . help me with the books. I'm Liam Capper, owner of Searchlight TV and deacon of the Church of the Lord's Holy Command."

"I'm Dak Sifter," I say, pretending not to notice that Wanda's hair is messed up and her blouse is now tucked into the waistband of her panties. Those books must be pretty hard to manage!

"So," says Liam, "you're here to interview for the delivery job. Normally, I hire only members of our church, but I'm in a bit of a pinch right now. So, tell me, do you love Jesus?"

"If people were more like Jesus," I say, "the world would be a better place."

I haven't been to church since I was nine-years-old, but I really do mean that. The kind, wise, forgiving Jesus I learned about in Sunday School seemed like someone worth looking up to.

"Do you walk in the light of the Lord, and obey his holy commands?" Liam Capper asks. The weird glow in his eyes tells me I had better not say no. Since I haven't yet had many opportunities to break any of the Ten Commandments, I, more-or-less, truthfully say, "Sure."

"Great!" says Liam Capper. "Just one more question — do you have a valid driver's license, and can you drive a large van?"

"Of course!" I say, confident in the knowledge that I have been practicing my driving in Mom's Honda Civic and, despite backing one tire over a curb while parallel parking, I did manage to pass my driver's test.

"Perfect!" says Liam Capper. "You're hired. You can start right now."

I work like a slave all day, loading dozens of heavy televisions into the Searchlight TV van without any help from Liam Capper, who spends most of the day loudly summoning Wanda into his office for more help with the books. The shock absorbers on the dilapidated delivery van are totally worn out. So compared to my Mom's Honda Civic, driving the bouncy cube van around town feels more like flying a helicopter through turbulence. The customers to whom I deliver goods all seem to be members of the Church of the Lord's Holy Command, judging by their frequent use of the phrase *Jesus forgive you*, and the ubiquitous long dresses, braids, and lack of makeup on the women. After a few deliveries, it begins to unnerve me how the women always look at their feet when men are present.

The strangest delivery of the day, though, is to the Church of the Lord's Holy Command itself. Reverend Rathburn requested a new television for his office, and deacon Liam Capper practically drools all over himself to oblige. Liam sends me to deliver the Reverend the best TV in the store, an enormous *real* Sony. I feel my muscle fibers tearing as I struggle to heft the huge television crate over the van's tailgate.

The church itself resembles a postmodern shopping mall — all white brick and stainless steel. On the wall nearest the building's entrance, a huge steel cross hangs with a jagged lightning bolt cutting through it. Beneath this symbol is a large plaque inscribed with the following words:

The Church of the Lord's Holy Command
Faireville District Parish
The Superior Reverend Ignaceous Rathburn, Presiding
"JESUS FORGIVE YOU"

Ignaceous Rathburn? Where had I heard that name before?

I walk inside feeling tense and jumpy which is a strange way to feel in a place of worship. At the end of a long corridor is a stainless steel door engraved with the cross-and-lightning logo and the words, Office of the Reverend. A couple sit in the plastic chairs to the right of the door — the man with his chest puffed out and his chin in the air, and the woman hunched over with her face cupped in her hands, her long skirt tucked between her legs. Maybe they can tell me where to drop off the television.

As I walk towards them, the steel door opens and out steps an enormous man with wiry, shoulder-length black hair and a jaw like a cement block. He is wearing shimmering, gunmetal-blue robes, with the cross-and-lightning logo embroidered in silver across his barrel-shaped chest. Large gold rings encircle each of his meaty fingers like brass knuckles. I stop in my tracks.

The man in the robes turns his elevated gaze upon the woman.

"Cynthia," his voice echoes through the hall, "according to your loving master Paul, there is a problem we need to address."

Now I remember where I've heard the name Ignaceous Rathburn — he had once been known as Iggy Wrath, former lead singer of the thrash-metal band Ejaculator, which fell off the public radar when a judge sentenced Iggy to an extended stay at a correctional facility.

The woman pleads, "But Reverend, it was an accident! I only — "

"You broke one of the Lord's holy commands!" Rathburn glowers.

"As I already explained to my loving master, I was only trying to — "

"THE LORD'S HOLY COMMANDS ARE NOT TO BE BROKEN!" Rathburn roars. He grabs her arm in one of his huge fists and jerks her from her seat. She hangs like a rag doll from his grip as he drags her through his office door and shoves her onto a sofa just inside the doorway. *"Jesus forgive me!"* the woman shrieks as

Reverend Ignaceous Rathburn kicks the door shut behind him.

Her husband sits there with his arms folded across his chest looking strangely smug.

I sprint out of the building, heave the television from the back of the van and shove it through the front doors of the church. I drive away with one side of my brain fearing what might be happening to that woman in the Reverend's office and the other side wondering if it's all just my imagination.

Later that evening, Zoe and I sit on the same side of a booth at the local burger joint comparing our notes for tomorrow's science test. I tell her that I'm saving for a car of my own and that I've just started a new job delivering TVs for Searchlight TV. I am just getting into the story of my weird visit to the Church of the Lord's Holy Command, when Zoe's jaw drops.

"The Church of the Lord's Holy Command?" she interrupts. "The *CLHC*? Haven't you been reading the papers or watching the news?"

"Zoe, I'm working two jobs and going to school. When do I have time to read the papers or watch TV?"

"Dak, if your new boss is involved with *them*, you've got to quit right away. They're more like a brainwashing cult than a church. It's been a running story in *The Star* for the past two weeks: 'Bad Men Who Love Jesus.'"

"Oh, come on, Zoe . . . as if anything that sinister is happening in Faireville! You can't even rent an R-rated movie in this town!"

"They've got these so-called churches popping up everywhere," Zoe continues. "They recruit new members from drug and alcohol rehab programs, unemployment offices, and other places where people are hurting and vulnerable. The FBI and the RCMP have been trying to get to them for years for tax evasion, fraud, and other illegal stuff, but they haven't been able to get enough evidence — the congregation members are intimidated into keeping their mouths shut, and the church insiders cover their tracks too well."

"I'm sure not all of them cover their tracks so well," I say, remembering the phony receipt Wanda left lying on the counter in full view.

"That's not even the worst part," Zoe continues. "The women are forced to submit completely to the men, and there's even an official dress code. The women are punished for exposing their legs or letting their hair down, or doing anything that might arouse lust in other men. Yet, they are supposed to do whatever the men of the church demand, whenever they demand it. They get punished if they refuse."

My stomach tightens as I tell Zoe about the woman who was dragged by Reverend Rathburn into his office, and the way her husband had watched with his head high in the air. I guess it wasn't just my imagination after all.

"God, Zoe," I say, "the crap people do to each other in the name of Jesus. It must really piss Him off."

"You can't go back there, Dak," Zoe says, inching a little closer to me on the vinyl bench seat and giving me the big brown eyes treatment. It never fails to make me to do whatever she asks. "These are dangerous people. Quit your job at the TV store. Promise me you won't go back."

During the week that follows, I take some time to scour the city newspapers for information about the Church of the Lord's Holy Command. There is nothing at all until Friday, when *The Star* prints an official apology and retraction for "alleged misinformation and innuendo" they printed earlier about the CLHC. In another major newspaper it is revealed that one of the CLHC deacons, who also happens to be a notorious litigation lawyer, is threatening *The Star* with a lawsuit.

The newspapers can't stop them. The police can't stop them. I go to bed with a feeling of powerlessness, like fingers of ice are closing around my heart. Tomorrow is Saturday, and I am supposed to show up for my second day of work at Searchlight TV. What am I going to do?

During the night, I have a strange and vivid dream. I am driving along in the Searchlight TV van, but gliding through the sky rather than bouncing along a road. Beside me in the passenger seat sits Jesus Christ, not the CLHC's version of Jesus, but the Jesus I knew and trusted when I was a little kid in Sunday School. He has never appeared in my dreams before, but here He is, nodding along to the blues playing on the van's radio. Jesus is speaking directly into my mind, saying, "Do what you have to do."

"I don't understand," I say out loud. "What do I have to do?"

The words Jesus sends back into my brain are, "When the time comes, you will know."

Then Jesus smiles and vanishes. The tires bounce against the ground with a jolt, and I sit upright in bed, my heart pounding.

It is six o'clock. I rise and dress. Despite my promise to Zoe, I am going back to Searchlight TV for a second Saturday. I hope that she will understand. There are greater forces at work here.

My first assignment of the day is a job I haven't done before. An elderly woman had been into the store the day before complaining of poor television reception. I am to climb up on her roof, replace her old antenna with an expensive, high-tech one, and replace the old flat antenna wire with coaxial cable. After I load the huge antenna, a toolbox, and a heavy spool of cable into the Searchlight TV van, Liam hands me a pre-printed bill and a cell phone.

"This is an important job," he says. "Call me if you have any problems."

When I arrive at the tiny bungalow where I am to install the new antenna, I can't resist peeking at the bill. Nine hundred bucks for a TV antenna? Two hundred for a roll of cable? *A three hundred and fifty dollar charge for labour?* Even at *double* minimum wage, Liam seems to be grossly overcharging for my services.

"Oh, I am so glad you're here!" says the lady who answers the door.

Her brown skin is creased with deep laugh lines, and from the small dot in the center of her forehead, I surmise that she is probably one of those rare Searchlight TV customers who doesn't attend the Church of the Lord's Holy Command. Perhaps this was why she is getting fleeced even worse than the suckers in Reverend Rathburn's congregation.

"My reception was very clear until a few days ago," she explains, "when it suddenly turned all snowy! Other than my kitten Ari, my television is the only company I have."

The lady and I walk around to the side of the little house, and I peer up at her old antenna. My eyes follow the line of flat wire down the side of the house, and then I see the problem. Near the ground, a kitten is batting at the wire that hangs disconnected from the house. Closer observation reveals that the kitten has probably chewed through the wire.

"Oh, Ari!" the lady gently scolds the kitten as she carries it inside, "you naughty little baby, you!"

I pull some slack wire from inside the house, use my jackknife to strip the casing back from the loose ends and twist the wire strands together. I double-wrap the repair with electrical tape from the toolbox, which hopefully will dissuade the kitten from chewing the wire again.

Inside the house, the television reception is crystal clear. The lady is very pleased and thanks me repeatedly.

The cell phone Liam gave me is a cheap Sany product that won't work inside the house. So I go back outside to inform him of my success.

"It turns out that she doesn't need a new antenna after all," I explain. "A kitten chewed through the antenna wire. I fixed it, and her reception is fine now. Should I just charge her a few bucks for my time?"

"No," Liam answers, "you were sent to replace her antenna and cable, and that is what you are going to do."

"But she doesn't need any of that stuff."

"She signed a *contract* for the stuff, so you are going to *install* it, and she is going to *pay* for it. Get her to pay *cash* if you can."

"This doesn't seem right, Liam. I don't think she has a lot of money."

"ARE YOU QUESTIONING MY AUTHORITY?" he thunders. "DO THE JOB I SENT YOU TO DO, OR I WILL . . . "

"*Jesus* wouldn't rip off an old lady," I say, and hang up the phone. It rings almost immediately. I switch it off.

I go back into the house and tell the lady there will be no charge for the repair. Then I drive back to Searchlight TV. As I walk in through the back door, my body is pulsing with angry blood, but I try to stay cool. Behind the closed door of his office, I can hear Liam Capper barking, "It is your *duty* to obey your loving master, Wanda, and *I* am your loving master! You *will* obey me!"

Without knocking, I push the office door open and walk in. Liam jumps out of his desk chair. Wanda, who is on her knees beside the desk, also jumps up, babbling, "Oh! Oh!" She runs from the room, her hands over her face to conceal her tears.

"What the hell are you doing back here so soon? I told you to . . . "

"I'm not ripping off an old woman, Liam."

"HOW DARE YOU!" he sputters, "I *COMMAND* YOU TO — "

"You can't *command* me to do anything, you crook. I *quit*. Pay me, and I'll be on my way."

"SCREW YOU, HEATHEN! I OWE YOU *NOTHING*!"

"I think the law might disagree with you, there, Liam."

"FINE!" he bellows. I guess he doesn't like the idea of the police poking around in his store. He throws himself onto his chair, scribbles out a cheque, and throws it in my direction.

"*Twenty bucks?*" I cry out. "*Twenty bucks* for fourteen hours work?"

Liam Capper leans back in his chair, grinning.

"Well," he says smugly, "we don't pay delivery employees for time spent on the road. And we don't pay for work done for the church since that's considered charity work. And we deduct two hours pay for lunch and dinner each day . . . "

"But I didn't take lunch or dinner breaks! And you never told me about any of that other stuff!"

"PROVE I didn't!" he says. He puts his feet up on his desk and folds his hands behind his head. "Now you better get out of here before I discover that you've been stealing from us."

"WHAT? I haven't — "

"Numbers on a computer are easy to change. I can make it look like stock suddenly began disappearing as soon as you started working here."

I tear up his cheque and toss the shreds on his desk.

"Keep your dirty money, you thief," I say.

"*Jesus forgive you!*" Liam calls out in a saccharine-sweet voice, as I stomp out the back door.

What I do next happens almost independent of my will, as if my body is on autopilot. It is like an outside force is guiding me along. It is almost like I'm dreaming.

I am walking towards home when I stop in the middle of the sidewalk. I spin and walk back to the front of Searchlight TV. When I peek through the store's front window, I can hear Liam calling loudly for Wanda. "I'm not finished with you, Wanda! Get back here!"

As Wanda drags herself into the backroom again, I step into the store and walk to the sales counter. From a ledge beneath the countertop, I pluck two computer disks, respectively labelled *Inventory and Sales – April (Gov't)* and *Inventory and Sales – April (CLHC)* — one set of books for the government, another set for the church. I slide the disks into my back pocket and leave the store. As simple as that.

It is a couple of weeks later, my parents are out of town, and Zoe is over at my place. Naturally, being alone for the evening we go straight to my bedroom — to read the newspaper. I have the sports pages and Zoe has the national news section.

"OH MY GOD!" she shrieks. "Listen to this!"

She begins reading out loud:

> *Bad Books Bring Down CLHC Ministry*
> *(Faireville - CP)*
> Liam Capper, a Faireville businessman with links to the Church of the Lord's Holy Command (CLHC) was arrested Monday in an early morning raid on his appliance store, Searchlight TV. Based on several anonymously sent computer disks containing incriminating evidence of tax evasion and fraud, police obtained warrants to search the premises.
>
> Upon entering the store, police allegedly discovered Mr. Capper engaged in abusive behaviour with an unnamed female employee, also a member of the CLHC. Mr. Capper then became violent, allegedly attacking a

police officer with a symbol of the CLHC — a steel cross with a lightning bolt. Police used force to subdue him.

The female employee later led police to further evidence of illegal activities by Capper and other deacons of the CLHC. She gave additional testimony concerning the long-suspected manipulative and abusive practices of the organization. Other female members of the congregation are said to be coming forth with testimony.

Police also searched the office of Ignaceous Rathburn, leader of the Faireville CLHC, and former singer of the punk rock band, Ejaculator. Rathburn, who has been linked to fraudulent activities documented in records from Searchlight TV, has apparently fled. His office was found emptied of all documents, frustrating attempts by investigators to further infiltrate the CLHC organization . . .

"I'll bet his wife got sick of being treated like a slave and sent those computer disks in herself," Zoe says.

"That would be poetic, wouldn't it?" I say.

I am considering telling her how the disks really got to the police, when Zoe says, "I'll bet you're glad I made you promise to never go back there, eh?"

She winks at me when she says that, and kisses my cheek. I feel a little twinge of guilt for breaking my promise, but I think I'll be forgiven for my transgression.

I look at the newspaper photo of an enraged Liam Capper as he is led to a police cruiser, his hands cuffed behind his back.

Jesus forgive you, Liam.

Cruisin' Machine

(Grade ten)

Some of the most significant memories in the hearts of men are their firsts. First dates, first kisses, first drinks, first voyages, and the first tastes of independence; they all represent great steps on the awkward climb to manhood. Today, all of these things seem within my reach. This afternoon, I will purchase my first car.

Unlike most of my buddies, I work weekends and evenings after school as an indentured servant of J.D.'s Gas-O-Rama. Needless to say, the wages are not overly generous, but through perseverance otherwise uncommon to my nature, I have managed to scrape together nine hundred big ones. To do this, I have had to greatly restrain the portion of my income which was normally dedicated to the necessities: rock albums, concert tickets, and twenty-dollar six-packs from Crazy Jack the bootlegger.

I have made many sacrifices, but I am a man with a mission. The focus of my existence has turned to the procurement of the big prize, and nothing is going to stop me. I want a car. And not just any car either. I picture myself behind the wheel of a snarling, snorting, tire-smoking, rock-and-rolling, hundred-and-sixty-mile-an-hour girl-magnet on wheels. I don't think it's too much to hope for.

Luckily, my dad was a street racer in the fifties, in his fondly remembered Ford Roadster, so I have an important ally in my quest for mobility. Mom has also grudgingly accepted my proposal, reasoning that I will be available to act as a personal chauffeur to my annoying thirteen-year-old sister, Charlotte (excuse me while I pause to laugh hysterically at Mom's naiveté). Naturally, all of my buddies are behind me as well — to scoop up the excess babes, no doubt. Everything is looking wonderful; I'm seeing the world through a rose-coloured windshield.

My desire for a cruising machine finally comes to a climax during Friday afternoon's math class — I'm so exited, I haven't been able to sleep a wink. As soon as the bell rings, I stride out the door and up the street to Virtuous Vic's Used Car Corral and Laundromat, my heart full of pride and my faded old Levi's stuffed with freshly withdrawn twenties.

The moment I pass under the flashing neon sign at the entrance, a greasy, slouching little man materializes in front of me, sporting three days' worth of facial hair and a sludge-encrusted baseball cap which reads *1989 Detroit Battle of the Monster Trucks*. Probably noticing the look of desperation on my face, he asks, "Kin I show yuh somethin', boy?"

"I want to buy a cruisin' ma . . . er, a car," I say with businesslike authority. "What have you got for under nine hundred dollars?"

"Nine hundred, eh . . . " he ponders, trying to look serious. "Howzabout that nice, clean, Chevrolet Chevette over there? It ain't got much rust, it's easy on the gas, and, uh, it's finished in a nice sporty red. It's got cool rally rims, too!"

A *Chevette*? I am deeply offended, and I wonder if this fellow is actually Virtuous Vic, or just some dumb employee who polishes the chrome (on those cars that actually have any). This guy is talking to me like I'm willing to settle for something reliable and economical! I'm not going to stand for such an insult and decide to show this clown just what kind of automotive man he's dealing with.

"Um, well, have you got anything with a little more, um . . . power?" I ask.

"Well, boy" he slowly and hoarsely whispers, stroking his chin as if deep in thought, "I got a lil' jobbie out back with more horsepower under the hood than a stray cat's got fleas . . . but I wouldn't sell that baby to just anybody." Then he turns and looks me straight in the eyes. "Do yuh think yuh got what it takes to handle a muscle machine like that? I mean, we're talkin' one badass vee-hicle here, boy."

It doesn't matter that the salesman's acting about as convincing as Woody Allen playing Darth Vader; it doesn't matter that the word "jobbie" is often used by my three-year-old cousin to describe the results of a successful session of potty training; it doesn't even bother me that I am about to put my life savings into the hands of a guy who likes monster trucks. I ignore all the omens. This is destiny.

My eyes narrow to slits, and my chest expands as I draw a deep breath; I feel like I'm the hero in a Hollywood action film, about to gun down the villain in the final climactic showdown. In my deepest post-pubescent voice, I speak the ominous words: "Let's have a look at it."

"It's out back," intones the salesman.

It is love at first sight (and we all know how blind love can be). It sits amidst the oil barrels and the overgrown weeds, staring at me provocatively with its twin sets of headlights, its grille sections formed in a sly, nasty grin. It is . . . Oh, it is sexy. I move in closer.

It is a '66 Pontiac Laurentian. Four doors. Metallic lime green. Great big sixteen-inch wheels. A trunk you could park a Chevette in. The entire Canadian Air Force could land on the hood. It has little gouges and scratches all over it, like a battle-scarred warrior, and angular, spear-like protrusions in the front that could rip through a Jeep like a hot bullet through a lump of lard. My heart races. I feel faint.

Suddenly, a voice cuts through my euphoria; "Well, whadda yuh think, boy? She may look a little rough on the outside, but under that there hood — whoo boy, she's wildfire!"

As if the subliminal imagery of referring to the car as a she isn't already more than my inflamed young hormones can handle, my shaggy-faced friend looks me straight in the eyes and delivers the final sales blow.

"There's a bonus involved here, boy."

What member of the human race can possibly resist a bonus?

"Now I know the thing on the side of the car says `V-8 289 C.I.' but it ain't got no wimpy little excuse of an engine like that," he explains. "Yep, she's got an over-hauled 454 inside. Was put in by the last owner with his own hands. That car there will blow them young mommas' boys in their Camaros right into next week!"

Although I've slept through quite a few math classes, I know that 454 is a much, much larger number than 289; I also relish the image of sending a few mommas' boys for a some unexpected time travel — particularly that weasel Jimmy Tanner. Naturally, when the salesman tells me I can drive away with this classic muscle car this very day, I practically throw my money at him.

The price, interestingly enough, comes to exactly nine hundred dollars and forty-six cents (including titles, taxes, fees, fuel allowances, licenses, and destination charges, whatever any of that means). As I sign on the dotted line, thanking him for letting me forget about the forty-six cents, I wonder exactly what the phrase AS IS on the contract means. As I thunder away in a great billow of blue-grey smoke and volcanic ash, I am too wrapped up in the enormity of my accomplishment to worry about it much.

Unfortunately, my illusions of fame and grandeur quickly disintegrate under the weight of reality. I'd figured that rolling into the school parking lot in my rumbling, backfiring, smoking, mobile road hazard would fill my life with adoring young females, but I've discovered that I actually met more girls when I rode the rumbling, backfiring, smoking school bus. My disillusionment is further amplified by the realization that the money I had previously used to support my weekend six-pack habit is now consumed by my car's insatiable appetite for gasoline, oil, and engine parts.

Now comes the final blow. Exactly three months have passed since I handed my money over to "Vermin" Vic, and as if to deliver the killing stroke to my critically wounded pride, it happens on the night of my first car date with Zoe Perry.

Zoe agreed to the date on two conditions: We cannot technically refer to the date as a date, since her soon-to-be ex-boyfriend Jimmy might object, and I have to promise that I won't get her killed on the way there, since I have managed to earn the dubious distinction of being the only guy in the recent history of Faireville High ever to accumulate seven speeding tickets in less than three months. Naturally, being the gentleman that I am, I drive at exactly the speed limit, even going so far as to slow down for stop signs and small children.

Zoe brushes a lock of her silky brown hair from of her face, puts her hand on my shoulder, and smiles at me as we pull up to a stoplight. Everything is going so well. Until, out of the corner of my eye, I see it.

It is a red Camaro. It is in the lane right beside us. And the guy behind the wheel is most certainly a momma's boy. He looks over at my grizzled Pontiac, and I swear I see him snicker. I have no choice. Road war has been declared.

I survey the Camaro to see what I am up against. The shiny gold letters on the side tell me that it is an I.R.O.C.

"Oh yeah, pal?" I say, more to Zoe than to the Camaro's driver. "My car's an I.R.O.C., too. The letters stand for `I Run Over Camaros.'"

The light turns green. I stomp on the accelerator, and my mighty combat machine lurches forward, the magnificent roar of its 454 engine overwhelms the Camaro's pitiful whine. My fingers grip the steering wheel and I stare straight ahead so confident and undaunted that I barely feel Zoe's fingernails digging into my arm.

The engine screams like a crazed warrior as the tachometer edges into the red. Slowly, I start pulling ahead of the Camaro. I am winning! I am winning! If I can just hang on to third gear for a few seconds longer I can —

KA-PLOOOOM!

The overwhelming sound of the mighty 454 exploding reverberates through the surrounding farmland. A valve stem shoots through the sheet metal of the hood and lands on the pavement with a sickening clatter.

An eerie silence follows. I feel as if an ice pick has been thrust through my heart.

Despite my horror, I manage to steer my disabled vehicle onto the gravel at the side of the road as it sputters and coughs and spews oily smoke from under the hood. Through tear-filled eyes, I watch the Camaro disappear into the distance.

In one fateful moment my dreams of fame, fortune, and of Zoe Perry grind to a sickening halt. My big race results in weeks of ridicule, courtesy of my buddies who go as far as to put an ad in the local paper for Dak's Automotive Demolition. I am also forced to suffer the humiliation of being rescued from the scene of devastation by my mom, who spends the trip back into town talking with Zoe, discussing the ridiculous facets of the male ego. I suffer from acute inferiority every time I see a Camaro. Worst of all, Zoe refuses to speak to me, and our study sessions are no more.

Everything I wanted had seemed within my reach. How could I have lost it all so easily?

Thank You, Quentin Alvinstock

(Grade eleven)

It's the second month of grade eleven, and my life totally sucks. I blew my savings on a car that now rests in pieces in the Faireville Wrecking Yard, and I am stuck riding the school bus with geeky grade nines and tens. I am helplessly in love with Zoe Perry, who acts as if I don't exist. My annoying sister is in grade nine, and she's doing better on the romantic front than I am. I might as well put myself out of my misery by joining a monastery.

The only small ray of sunshine in my otherwise dark world is that I did not get stuck in my father's grade eleven English composition class. Instead, I've got the new guy, Quentin Alvinstock. As high school teachers go, he's a pretty good guy, other than being in desperate need of effective underarm deodorant. Mr. Alvinstock prefers to teach books like *Catch 22*, *Slaughterhouse Five*, and *The Catcher in the Rye*, unlike my father, who feeds his students a strict diet of Shakespeare and Robertson Davies. Dad is now the head of the English Department at Faireville High. He calls the ex-hippie Mr. Alvinstock a slacker and a pinko, and is desperate to find a reason to rid his English Department of such a menace. So naturally, I've decided to give Quentin Alvinstock a chance.

At first, I hold it against him that he is making all of us write a poetry mini-collection for part of our term mark. Asking an average grade eleven guy to write at least four meaningful poems is, as school assignments go, nearly equivalent to asking my sister to have a telephone conversation with one of her giggly little friends in fifty words or less.

"Oh, man," I moan, "not poetry! Anything but poetry!"

This is a comment that would get me thrown out of my own father's writing class, but Mr. Alvinstock just chuckles and says, "Well, Dak — and any of you other gentlemen who feel the same way — poetry is often an effective means of communicating our feelings to members of the opposite sex." We interpret this to mean that poetry will get us laid. And, of course, we are all okay with that!

"Write from your heart!" Mr. Alvinstock sings out. "Write what you know! Write what you feel! Write about the tiniest, most beautiful details you've noticed! Write about the biggest things you've experienced in life! Write, write, write!"

So, I write, write, write. There doesn't seem to be much choice about it, really, considering Mr. Alvinstock is basing a hefty chunk of our term mark on it. Besides, it isn't too difficult to peg down my biggest experience as of late. I only have to look as far back as the end of summer, just before school started.

Thank You, Quentin Alvinstock

SOMETHING TO TALK ABOUT ON THE FIRST DAY BACK
AT FAIREVILLE DISTRICT HIGH SCHOOL, GRADE ELEVEN

It was Saturday
I washed my car
Drove up and down the dock past the ice cream bar
See and Be Seen
It was the Summertime Law

Billy called shotgun
Ray back with Dean
Cranked down the windows
Turned up The Max Machine
One-arm-suntan-poses
Were critical

Beach and ocean
Through a rose-coloured windshield
Sun-bronzed bodies
Like wheat in a sand field
If I dare to touch one
Will she die in my hands?

Every day like a pop song
All backbeat, no danger
I steer with my knees
and dream safely of strangers
Speakers thump out bravado
(It's critical)

The last night of August
When Summertime ends
She leans through my window
It's half-past ten
No longer pretending
(It's critical)

She says "Let's go to the boardwalk"
I say "okay"
The buzz of the radio
And seagulls and waves
I 've got beers in the trunk in a cooler
(Also critical)

My heartbeat thunders
Deep in my ears
It may be passion
It may be fear
The boys will wonder why I was late
I don't know what I'll say

Okay, so I stole the rhythm from a tune on an old Joe Walsh album, but I'm still kind of pleased with the way it turned out. And I guess the cool thing is that I didn't tell anyone, not even Billy or Dean, about what happened that night, which makes the title sort of ironic (which might have got me a higher mark from Mr. Alvinstock if he'd known). Why didn't I tell my buddies about the one occurrence which almost every guy in the history of grade eleven lies about experiencing? Well, I have my reasons.

I am more in love with Zoe Perry than ever. At first it was her stunning beauty which drew me in, but after engineering a few study sessions with her in grades nine and ten, I came to realize that she has more than enough intelligence, wit, and personality to match her appearance, and my attraction to her has increased exponentially (even if I have become a little afraid that she might be too good for me). Alas, because of the exploding Pontiac incident during our first and only car date in grade ten, Zoe has decided that I am the biggest geek on the planet, and she has fallen out of the habit of speaking to me on a regular basis — or at all, actually. She occasionally rolls her eyes and shakes her head when I say something stupid in class while trying to be funny, but mostly she just pretends that she doesn't know me.

It hurts me terribly, but fortunately, I have rented *Casablanca* several times and I'm still in with the local bootlegger, so I've been following Bogey's example and drinking my sorrows away. I'm sure even the heart-broken Humphrey Bogart barfed a few times — off camera, of course.

Anyway, Zoe has continued dating that phony-baloney pretty boy Jimmy Tanner. Jimmy has enough hairspray in his salon-perfect hairdo to have his own personal hole in the ozone layer. He wears a pretentious looking trench coat and has a bristly little goatee, and he always walks around with his eyebrows arched as if he either knows something the rest of humanity doesn't, or else he's been the first to smell another person's fart. For some reason, the girls at school all believe that this puffed-up pansy is some sort of Casanova. Yet, rather than throwing a banana peel under his immaculately polished shoes (which, admittedly, is the only idea I had for a while), I have decided to beat him at his own game and learn everything there is to know about pleasuring a woman.

I read the letter sections in the skin magazines I borrowed from my uncle's garage in grade seven. I read all of the books my mom kept carefully hidden at the bottom of her underwear drawer. I secretly exercise my tongue and lips while chewing gum. I even go so far as to drive to another town to buy a pack of those special ribbed-for-her-pleasure condoms. When Zoe finally comes to her senses and dumps Jimmy Tanner, I am going to be ready to satisfy her every need.

G·G·G·

Right at the end of summer, an opportunity presented itself for me to put all of my studies and endurance training to the test.

I was cruising up and down the beach in my crummy old rust-perforated pickup, looking for a quiet, unpopulated place to pop a beer, watch the sun go down, and pretend that I was the hero in a forties movie who could take it like a man. I was making a U-turn just in front of the Faireville Docks, the town's most popular outdoor pickup spot, when she waved me over. Winifred Bright. The legendary Winifred Bright.

Winifred Bright lives in one of the apartments above one of the little stores in downtown Faireville. She is considered the Devil's representative when the sins of the flesh are discussed in hushed tones by Faireville's tea-and-cookie social elite. Because she is thirty-two-years old and still single. Because she embraces the people in Faireville who others try to ignore. Because many years ago she spent some time in a mental institution dealing with depression. Because she allegedly had a daughter named Robin, who was sent away during Winifred's time in the mental hospital. But mostly, Winfred Bright is the object of their scorn because she does not attempt to hide any of this.

Whenever the teenaged daughter of a town busybody is caught in the act of kissing a boy in a car (or some similar atrocity) a finger is pointed invariably in the direction of Winifred Bright as an example of what happens to girls who offer their affections indiscriminately. I suppose Winifred eventually decided to accept the role in which the more tightly wound townsfolk had cast her, because she slinks down the sidewalk in plastic wrap pants, and loose, low-cut blouses that allow for much jiggling and bouncing. She has the type of physique that inspires certain men to lean out through the windows of their rusting, hubcap-free vehicles, and hoot "Whew-wee! Would'ja lookit THAT!"

Most of her time is spent atop a barstool in a dark corner of The Outpost, a windowless, stucco-splattered watering hole about two miles outside the town limits. Most non-clients refer to bar as The Outhouse, a fairly accurate moniker considering the bar's clientele. Winifred brings a man home from the bar nearly every night, and, according to rumour (nobody will admit to having discovered this first-hand) Winifred never demands anything in exchange for a night in her bed. Also according to gossip, she is fond of initiating boys into manhood, although I can personally attest that I felt no nearer to manhood afterward than I did before. In fact, after it was over, I felt a little smaller, a little more overwhelmed by the world.

Everybody in Faireville knows that Winifred has posters of Chairman Mao Tse Tung plastered all over the walls of her apartment. It isn't that anyone has ever been there, of course — you can see them from the street at night. Winifred rarely bothers to lower her blinds; some say that this is a clever advertising technique. Whenever the Beatles' tune "Revolution" gets played on the radio, certain righteous citizens of Faireville figure jokingly that the Beatles never knew Winifred Bright, because she owns pictures of Chairman Mao, yet she makes it with practically everyone, anyhow. Others scratch their heads and wonder aloud just who in the world Mousy Tongue is.

Her reply to such queries is usually a version of this statement: "Mao Tse Tung is a man who said that we should all work together, that we should share our talents and our gifts with our fellow human beings." I really don't know if Chairman Mao said anything like that, but maybe it doesn't matter that much. People believe what they want to believe.

Anyway, I stopped the truck halfway through a U-turn in front of the Docks, and Winifred Bright leaned through the open driver's side window of my truck, in a way that allowed the maximum amount of cleavage to burst forth from her scoop-necked top. Smiling slyly, she asked me if I knew who she was.

I told her that I thought I might have met her before.

She asked me if I would mind giving her a ride home.

I told her I was going to the beach, not back downtown.

She said she wouldn't mind coming along for the ride.

I told her I was in love with someone, and that I probably shouldn't.

She looked me straight in the eyes and said, "So, I guess you have nothing to learn then, eh?"

I didn't protest when she walked around the front of the truck and climbed into the cab with me.

She laughed later when I asked her if she enjoyed the ribbed-for-her-pleasure condom. She touched my hand and said, "It wasn't just the condom. You are going to make that *someone* feel wonderful."

Then she offered a strange, faraway grin, got out of the truck and walked away into the night. I sat in the truck for the rest of the night, the sound of the surf filling my ears, staring at the moonlit glow of my knuckles hanging from the steering wheel. I had expected to feel larger, more manly, more secure, more knowing, but it was the exact opposite. It was the world that seemed a lot bigger, a world filled with many more questions than answers.

C·C·C·

Since then, I've gone back to my old habit of admiring Zoe, mostly from a distance, like I'm doing right now in Mr. Alvinstock's English composition class. I'm thinking about Zoe in ways I couldn't have even imagined a few months earlier, and I'm wondering how many things *she* knows which I still don't. Women always seem to be two or three steps ahead of us guys, and it's a bit unnerving sometimes. This makes me feel like a small child lost in a dense, noisy jungle, so I mentally downshift and decide to simply admire certain points of interest beneath the folds of Zoe's William Shakespeare caricature T-shirt. Then an idea comes to me, which stretches and grows into a poem. I know rhyming isn't cool, but this is what I've written:

GREAT UNANSWERED QUESTIONS OF HISTORY

I wonder if Shakespeare was ever eighteen
Did he work at a gas bar, tell stories for free?
Did he hike to the East side to the beatnik cafe?
To hide in the shadows and drink underage?

I wonder when Plato got his first kiss
When she offered her lips, did he pucker and miss?
Did he make up tall tales to tell loafers at school?
Did he put on black leather, pretend to be cool?

I wonder if Einstein ever worried about
The zits on his face, while he made out
Had the cops in the campground heard the noise in the
tent?
Had he saved enough money for his college rent?

I wonder if Freud got weak in the knees
When a girl like you began to tease
Would you be there beside him when he woke up?
Would you head for the sunset with him in his pickup
truck?

Here tomorrow, gone today
History seems to work that way
Here today, just you and me
As for history, we'll just wait and see

My muse has found me! And she returns again, just as that fuzz-chinned, trench coat-wearing weasel Jimmy Tanner goes strutting past me in the cafeteria, with his nose held high like he's doing the air a favour by inhaling it. This is the final version:

STUNT MAN

Unlike the moving picture
Projected on that silver cloth
Who plays the lover's role
Who plays the hero's part

There's no need here for a mannequin
With plastic hair and breasts
To complete a movie still
Behind a plate of plastic glass

Won't see me in a tailored trench coat
Playing dress-up debonair
Blowing smoky movie promises
As the camera lens inhales

But when the script calls for your body to
Thrash helpless through the air
And the leading man can't take the risk
of messing up his hair

141

The stunt man will be me
I'll be there

Neatly transcribed in my best handwriting (which is only slightly more decipherable than ancient hieroglyphics), I drop a copy of this poem on the floor beside Zoe's desk (ooops!) as I brush past her in English composition class. I hope she'll pick it up, read it, and realize that I am the man for her. Alas, she doesn't even look at it, or at me.

So, between bouts of self-pitying boozing while sitting in the back of my crummy pickup at the beach, I wait. For weeks it feels as if I am holding my breath under water. I wait, with all of my new sexual knowledge and experience coiled up inside me like red-hot magma, bubbling beneath the surface, straining to erupt. I wait for the moment when Zoe Perry will finally release it all, and for the moment that will change forever the landscape of our lives, with explosion after explosion of ecstasy.

In the meantime, though, my hands are getting pretty calloused.

Mr. Alvinstock finally returns our graded poetry assignments. I get a B+ along with the comment, "The rhyming poems are pretty predictable, but I like the last one — Nice. Different."

Our fearless (if somewhat fragrant) teacher asks each of the students who have earned an A or A+ to come to the front of the class to read their poems. Zoe is one of them. Her poems are about the beauty of the things that surround us all the time, which most people never

bother to notice. Her words describe the Victorian build-
ings in our little town, the scents and sounds of the
beach, the slow motion fireworks of the sunsets, and the
thick, scented forests just outside of town. Her voice
trembles slightly as she reads. Surprisingly enough, Mr.
Alvinstock loves this kind of stuff — just write about
forests, and beaches, and old houses, and you're practically guaranteed an A+ from Quentin. Yet, even if Zoe's
poems are a lot like the ones the other kids in our class
write, the sound of her voice gets right inside me. Her
delivery is so clear and musical, her conviction so real,
that I can't look at her face for fear of a tear working its
way loose in front of all the guys.

"Wonderful work, Zoe, wonderful," Mr. Alvinstock
says, nodding and stroking his chin, his eyes glazing
over as Zoe returns to her seat. Is it possible that Mr.
Alvinstock also thinks Zoe is gorgeous? He clears his
throat. "Anyone else want to share their work?"

"Yeah," I say, my voice unexpectedly and ridiculously
cracking. "I'll do one."

"How interesting," Mr. Alvinstock says, "our most
vociferous anti-poet wants to share his words with us.
Please, Dak, share!"

A few of the guys snicker, but I don't care. At this
particular moment, there is no one else in the room but
Zoe. I look right at her as I clear my throat and read:

INVITATION

You tell me
You grew up in a town
Where smiles disguised intentions

You tell me
You were brought up in a house
Where dreams were never mentioned

This is an open invitation
to come as you are
no need to dress up or down
no need to make a reservation
to dance without light
to drink all the night
from the shadows

We can tango through
this rainy syncopation
with heartbeats as strong and steady
as ritual drums

This is your invitation
To dream
With me

When I say the last two lines, I catch Zoe's eyes for just a moment. Then she looks down at her desk, pretending for the remainder of the class to be examining the glowing comments written in red on the back page of her own poetry assignment. She doesn't even once glance across the room at me after I return to my desk.

But she has a smile on her face.

And for that, Mr. Quentin Alvinstock, I thank you.

Renaissance Man
(Grade eleven)

I cannot quite believe what I have just seen: My sister Charlotte has gone skipping from the living room with a cheque for six hundred dollars in her hand. The cheque was signed and handed over by my father with no resistance whatsoever; in fact, Dad said, "Have fun, Charlie!" as he handed over the money.

What the hell is going on? It normally takes a crowbar and a stick of dynamite just to get Dad's wallet open to pay the paper boy, so naturally I'm wondering how Charlotte has pulled this off. Is she practicing witchcraft? Voodoo? Or has poor Dad finally snapped after all those years of teaching English to the idiots at our high school?

I decide to get to the bottom of this abnormal behaviour. I creep up beside Dad, who is sitting in his favourite armchair behind a newspaper, and I test him with a simple question:

"Hey, Dad . . . Can I borrow some money to buy a new battery for my truck?"

"Very funny!"

"Well, um, you wouldn't want me stuck in the middle of nowhere because my truck wouldn't start, would you?"

"I guess you'd better stay away from the middle of nowhere then, eh?" he grumbles, without lowering his paper.

Well, this is a pretty normal response. Clearly, Dad is still his usual self. So what has Charlotte done to get so much cash out of Dad's fanatically guarded reserve? I march upstairs to her bedroom to confront her.

"Ever knock, Jerkweed?" she says as I walk into a bedroom wallpapered with magazine photos of the androgynous pretty boys popular with girls her age. She is lying on her stomach on the bed, poring over a brainless teen magazine.

"Are you bribing Dad?" I demanded. "Did you catch him having an affair or something?"

"What the hell are you talking about?"

"How did you get six hundred bucks out of Dad?"

"It's none of your business, Moron."

"So, you are bribing him! Who's he having the affair with?"

Charlotte rolls her eyes way back into her skull, as she does every time she is forced to converse with me.

"Well, *Doofus*, if you were the one *stuck* with the smaller bedroom next to Mom and Dad's room, you'd be the one to hear their stupid headboard banging against the wall every other night. So, obviously Mom and Dad are doing okay — or do I need to explain it to you?"

Oooooh. I hate it when the little brat talks to me like this, as if I'm the younger, dumber sibling!

"Listen, Charlie," I wheeze, just to piss her off (she hates being called Charlie, but she lets Dad do it since it seems to be in her financial interests), "what did Dad give you six hundred bucks for?"

"To get an abortion, okay!" she shrieks, and buries her face in the pillow.

I am dumbstruck. A lump sticks in my throat. My little sister is pregnant? She's only in grade nine. Oh, the poor little thing! No wonder she's so hostile. My fists clench. I will KILL the son of a bitch who . . .

Charlotte rolls over, throws her head back and begins to laugh hysterically, kicking her feet in the air.

"You're such a sap. I'm not pregnant — I wouldn't let any of the geeks in this town touch me! The money's for a course I'm signing up for. Not that it's any of your business."

"A course?"

"Yeah, a course, idiot. I'm taking an art history course."

"Art history? Since when did you care about anything but boy bands?"

"That's more or less what Dad said, too, until I convinced him that the course would help me get a job as a tour guide at the art gallery this summer."

Maybe Charlotte is on to something. Being a tour guide can't be all that difficult, and it could prevent Dad from shipping her off to work at the pickle factory, like he did with me a few summers ago. I envy her craftiness, so I respond the only way I know how:

"A tour guide? You couldn't find your armpit with a map and a flashlight! Though, if they want to hire a total idiot tour guide so the tourists will feel really smart in comparison, then . . . !"

"Then, you had better enrol right away, dickwad. Besides, that girl you like just started working at the art gallery," she says tauntingly, as if liking a girl is something that will embarrass me.

"What girl?"

"You know, the one you drool over, who thinks you're a total dork. The one you took on that romantic date where you blew up your car."

"Zoe Perry? Zoe works at the art gallery?"

"God, Dak, put your tongue back in your mouth!"

My sister wishes she'd kept her mouth shut when I ask Dad if I too can have six hundred bucks to take the art history course. Cleverly, I ask him while my grandparents are visiting, so that rather than risk appearing biased against my cultural education and favouring my sister, Dad is forced to fork over the money.

"You'll drive your sister, of course," Dad says with a tight-lipped grin.

Charlotte is outraged, and out of earshot of our parents and grandparents, she forbids me to sit near her or talk to her during the classes. Fine by me!

Three weeks later, after two hours a night every Monday and Thursday, I pass the final exam and am awarded my Certificate of Achievement from the Faireville Community Learning Centre. As far as academic credentials go, the certificate might as well be printed on a sheet of toilet paper, but it serves my purpose. The next morning I drive to the Faireville Gallery of Reproduction Masterpiece Art, brimming over with fresh artistic knowledge. Needless to say, I leave my sister at home — as if she'd have a chance at beating me for the job anyway.

A sign taped to the gallery's glass door reads: "Tour Guide Wanted: Knowledge of Art History Essential!" I carefully pull the sign off, fold it into quarters, and slip it into my back pocket. No further applicants need apply!

"Hello-o-o!" My voice echoes through the gallery's front hallway, which is filled with plaster replicas of famous sculptures, an impressive selection of prints, and some reasonably good forgeries of famous paintings. While waiting for a non-plaster human figure to appear, I pause to read the gallery's dedication plaque:

> The Faireville Gallery of Reproduction Masterpiece Art was opened on December 29, 1971, with the mandate of making the great works of the Ancient, Classical, and Renaissance Eras accessible to our fair town's citizens and tourists.
>
> The gallery's continued operation is made possible by a self-perpetuating donation made in trust by Jeremiah Faire III, Owner and CEO, The Krispy Green Pickle Company

Well, well. The energy from some poor sap's pickle pushing efforts at Krispy Green has been indirectly transformed into reproduction artworks for the citizens of Faireville to enjoy. I glance down at the scar on my wrist, which I earned during my first and only day as a Krispy Green employee. It now looks like a little pink caterpillar.

Maybe the few hundred jars of pickles I managed to help fill at the factory pushed the owner's annual earnings a few dollars into a higher tax bracket, and as a result of a deduction-seeking donation, there is now another fake Manet hanging in the gallery. The world works in strange ways.

A small group of elderly people shuffles into the far end of the gallery's main hallway, led by Zoe. She's wearing a green jacket with the gallery's logo on the lapel, and a matching skirt that clings to her legs six inches above her knees. My heart skips a beat.

"If you look to your left as we pass through the hallway," Zoe explains to the group, "you will see several beautifully reproduced examples of Greek sculpture from several different periods of history. The earliest, on the pedestal beside us, is a Kore, a sculpture of a female figure."

She sees me, nods, and raises her voice a little.

"The particular Kore from which this example was copied, was made during what is known as the Archaic Period of Greek art. An interesting fact about Greek sculpture in this early period is that it was very generic — practically all human figures carved at this time had the same facial expression — the tight-lipped, enigmatic smile which you see in front of you. They call it the Archaic Smile."

She has a similar expression on her own face as she once again glances in my direction.

"Of course," she continues, as she leads the tour group into an adjacent room, "this changed dramatically as Greek artists later entered a more expressive period of creation known as the Classical Era. Reproductions of several famous sculptures from this period appear to your left . . . "

Wow. Zoe's voice could make a reading from the Faireville phone directory sound like a symphony.

During the time it takes Zoe to return, I examine the reproductions in the main hallway, most of which I recognize from the course I've just finished. In twenty-two minutes (I've been checking my watch) Zoe is back in the main hallway without the tour group.

"Hey, Sifter," she says, "what are you doing here?"

"I'm here to apply for a job as a tour guide."

"Whoa. First poetry, now art. You're becoming a real Renaissance Man."

I like where this is going.

"Did you like the poem I read in class the other day?" I ask hopefully.

She forms one of those unreadable archaic smiles, and evades the question with another.

"What do you know about art history anyway?"

I pull my toilet paper certificate from my pocket and unfold it for her to see.

"Hmm. I'm impressed. But you'll have to impress Hilda if you want to be a tour guide here."

"And Hilda would be?"

"Hilda's the curator. My boss, and . . . " (her voice drops to a whisper) "she's also the most incredible bitch I've ever met. She screams at me over the slightest thing! Yesterday, she threw a fountain pen at me for mispronouncing Caravaggio! She's a friggin' Nazi!"

I picture in my mind what Hilda must look like: greying, brassy blonde hair pulled into a tight, scalp-numbing bun, her drab green business suit fitting as sexless as a military stenographer's uniform. Hilda, the female Gestapo officer. Then my vision of Hilda disappears as Zoe sits atop the desk and crosses her lovely legs while my own legs nearly buckle beneath me.

"You'll be able to handle Hilda, though," Zoe says. "She likes young men."

Hilda is not who I want to handle at the moment. It occurs to me that someone should do a sculpture of Zoe's legs, or perhaps her entire nude body. But I try to purge the thought from my head before there's further blood relocation.

A sweet, grandmotherly voice with an English accent sings out from behind us:

"Miss Perry! Tsk tsk! You shouldn't be cavorting with young gentlemen while on duty!"

Zoe leaps from the desktop, her heels skittering across the floor. I spin on my heels to face a smiling, portly woman with rosy cheeks and bifocal glasses. She is dressed in a floral pastel smock, and she is dipping a tea bag into a delicate china cup. She smells like marshmallows. She reminds me of my Kindergarten teacher.

"Please be a good girl and have your boyfriend run along now, dear."

"He's not my boyfriend," Zoe stammers, "well, he's sort of . . . he's a . . . ," she shrugs in my direction, looking desperate. "His name is Dak Sifter. He's here to apply for a job as a tour guide."

"Ah," Hilda says, sizing me up over the rims of her tiny spectacles. "You want to be a guide, do you, Mr. Sifter?"

I grin sheepishly and nod.

"And why do you want to be a tour guide, young man?"

I feel as if she can see right inside my head, that she somehow knows that I want to be a tour guide just so I can spend each day watching Zoe's short skirt shift back and forth as she walks. Nevertheless, I hold my art course certificate out for Hilda's perusal.

"Ah," she sighs happily, scrutinizing the cheap certificate with her plump chin raised high. "A scholar of the arts — rare in young men these days. Very well then, Mr. Sifter. You may give the next tour of the gallery — a bus is scheduled to arrive any moment. I will observe and Miss Perry can help out if necessary. Agreed?"

"Oh, yes," I say, "agreed!"

The phone rings in Hilda's office.

"Oh!" Hilda, says, scurrying away, "I've been expecting a call about a copy of a Renoir we've been after — excuse me, please. I'll join your tour in progress."

As soon as the latch on Hilda's office door has snapped closed, Zoe clicks her heels together and salutes, "Hail Hilda!"

"What?" I shrug. "She seems nice enough to me."

"Ever notice how all the psychopathic killers in movies have English accents just like hers? It's not coincidental. Did you know she has a print from Dante's *Inferno* hanging in her office, of a man being dragged down to hell? Once, during one of her rages, she picked up a fake Ming vase, and she — "

Zoe is interrupted as another tour group from the local retirement home shuffles in from their bus. She grins and says, "Good luck, Artmeister. You're on."

Full of Zoe-inspired bravado, I bounce out in front of the new arrivals, my voice booming as if I've just been possessed by a game show announcer.

"Good evening, folks, and welcome to The Faireville Gallery of Reproduction Masterpiece Art! I'm your host, Dak Sifter! We are going to take an exciting trip through the fun-filled world of reproduction masterpiece art!"

A few sweet-old-grandmother types in the crowd clap their hands. Zoe grins and shakes her head. The group follows me into the first chamber of the gallery as I look for paintings and sculptures I recognize from my Introduction to Western Art textbook.

"Let's start in 1425 with Masaccio's *Holy Trinity*, which depicts everybody's favourite deity, God, hobnobbing with the socialites who paid for the painting. And who says it doesn't pay to support the arts?! Just like our own hometown hero, Jeremiah Faire the third, who paid for the gallery we're standing in right now!"

The seniors are obviously locals because they applaud upon hearing Faire's name — most of them probably shared the same one-room schoolhouse with Jeremiah the first. Zoe applauds as well.

"And check this out!" I cheer, as I bounce over to the next painting, "it's *The Nativity, Between the Donors and Their Patron Saints*, which again shows the guys who paid for the painting hobnobbing with the Virgin Mary, Baby Jesus, and some of the better-heeled saints. What a crowd, eh? It was painted by Van Der Goes, and it *goes* well with any church altar!"

Zoe groans. The old people on the tour smile content-edly. I could probably be singing "Blue Suede Shoes" for all they care — they are happy to be anywhere other than the retirement home.

"And here's *La Primavera* by Botticelli. Ol' Botticelli was really into women with tiny bosoms and large bellies and bottoms. Guys like him could put all of the diet gurus and breast implant surgeons in the world out of business, eh?"

Zoe leans towards me and says, "Botticelli would have liked Hilda, eh?"

Her comment is unfortunately timed, as Hilda peeks around a partition just as Zoe speaks. Hilda frowns, jots a note down on a clipboard, then disappears again.

"But seriously folks," I continue, "how about that Leonardo Da Vinci? Was he a great talent or what? I mean, *The Last Supper*? *Mona Lisa*? Need I say more? So let's hear it for Da Vinci, and for the Early Renaissance! He was so cool that he once even travelled though time to appear on an episode of *Star Trek: Voyager*!"

The seniors clap happily.

"People loved the Early Renaissance so much they made a sequel: the High Renaissance! And these guys were good. Take Michelangelo, for example — he could sculpt *and* paint! If you'll be so kind as to look above your heads, you'll see The Faireville Gallery's painstak-ingly detailed copy of the ceiling of the Sistine Chapel."

One tiny lady says, "Oooooh!" Another squints and says, "I don't see it!"

I look up at the ceiling again, squinting.

"Whoops! Sorry folks. My mistake! That's not a repro-duction of the ceiling of the Sistine Chapel — it's actu-ally water-stained stucco."

Zoe giggles. A few of the tourists titter along with her. One of the old ladies says to Zoe, "He's cute!" I wait a moment for Zoe to agree, but she just rolls her eyes at me.

I march my followers through to the next gallery.

"Next came the Rococo style of painting, which depicted dandy, pasty-faced courtiers in breeches, flit-ting around fluffy treed and fluffy clouded courtyards with sweet, frail, porcelain maidens. This style was very popular with swishy, inbred French monarchs, but has a negative effect on important current art critics — namely, me. It is similar to eating a truckload of cotton candy. Yechhh! The main artist of this style was Fragonard, who was eventually hung by the neck until he died. Or at least that's what *should* have happened."

Hilda steps into the gallery again at this point, nodding her head in agreement. Apparently, she dislikes the Rococo style as well. Behind the tour group, Hilda follows us into the next room, and I am torn between wanting to make Zoe laugh and wanting to impress Hilda.

"Then came the Neo-Classical style," I continue, raising a hand dramatically each time I stroll past a painting. "It was a hard-edged, historically themed method which rebelled against the fluffy genre scenes of the Rococo technique. Next came the more emotional and patriotic Romanticism, which rebelled against the austerity of Neo-Classicism."

Hilda leaves the room, smiling and jotting a note on her clipboard. Time to make jokes again!

"Then there was Realism," I continue, "which depicted everyday people and things, and which rebelled against both Neo-Classicism and Romanticism, and threw rotten eggs at Rococo. Then a guy named Bob O'Toole-Flanagan came along and rebelled against everybody by hanging stuff other than paintings on his walls, such as farm implements, traffic signs, and car parts. And, thus, the North American restaurant franchise industry was born."

"Anyway, these next few paintings are by the Impressionists, whose leader was Monet. There was also another Impressionist named Manet. It's kind of like having another talk-show host called David Betterman, eh?"

Zoe giggles.

"After the Impressionists," I explain, "came the Pre-Cubists, who intentionally stuck to simple forms — cubes, cones, and spheres, and ignored the rules of mathematical perspective. So, cheer up all of you who are taking introductory oil painting! You're not lousy painters, you're Pre-Cubists!"

Zoe laughs out loud.

"We're Pre-Cubists, Doris!" one lady chirps to another.

Zoe is giggling uncontrollably, now. This is great! Working here with her is going to be so much fun!

At the end of the tour, back at the gallery's entrance, Hilda smiles warmly and extends a hand.

"Congratulations, Mr. Sifter! The bits of your tour I was able to see were very well done. Can you start working here on Monday morning? On a trial basis, of course."

"Of course!" I reply. From behind Hilda, Zoe leans against the reception desk and gives me a thumbs-up.

As if she has eyes in the back of her head, Hilda spins around and says, "Now, Miss Perry, dear, what have I told you about sitting on the desk? The desk is not a chair, dear!"

"I wasn't sitting, Hilda. I was only leaning."

Hilda's tone of voice immediately shifts into a bulldog snarl, as she stomps toward Zoe. "Leaning on a desk is just as unbecoming as sitting, Miss Perry," she snaps, "especially when one wears skirts as short as those you seem to favour." Hilda glances over her shoulder at me, her voice resuming its grandmotherly sweetness, and says, "Rather unladylike, I'm afraid. Attracts the wrong sort of boys, too, I might add. Don't you agree, Mr. Sifter?"

"Ahh . . . Ummmmm . . . Hmmm," is my response.

Ouch. Maybe Hilda is not so nice after all.

On Monday I return to the gallery for my first day as a tour guide.

In my pocket, as part of my plan to win Zoe again, is a poem I have written for her, which I am going to slip into her hand when the perfect moment presents itself. It begins:

GALLERY
(by Dak, for Zoe)

This woman wears an Archaic Smile
It doesn't change - I've been watching for awhile
It's just a convention of the times
And it nicely masks whatever's happening inside

She's gone, she's lost,
She's wasted on the post-modern eye
Only the sculptor knows for sure
What she was thinking at the time

And here she is again, the symbolic bride
Two thousand years have passed and she still averts her eyes
The Renaissance has veiled her in drapes of wine
But you'll have to call her Venus if you want her to recline

She's gone, she's lost
She's wasted on the Nintendo mind
Only the painter knows for sure
What drew him to her at the time

Monday's admission to the Gallery is free
There's one specific work I always come to see
She wears a nametag, and she gives the tour
These are the only things I know of her for sure

Is she gone? Lost?
Wasted in a digital age?
Is she the kind of poetry
Whose meaning lies beyond the page?

I want so much to give this poem to Zoe, to see her unfold it in her hands. It's practically burning a hole in my pocket. I want to be Zoe's Renaissance Man.

I walk through the entire gallery but Zoe is nowhere to be found. I knock on the door of Hilda's office and gently push the door open.

"Oh! Good morning, Mr. Sifter!" Hilda chirps, sitting upright behind her desk, dipping a tea bag into her china cup. "Come in! Come in!"

"Good morning, Hilda. So, um, during my trial period, will I, um, be working with a partner?"

"Oh, of course, dear," Hilda coos. She takes a sip from her teacup. "I would never leave a new tour guide all on his own."

"Um, well, will I be working with Miss Perry, then?"

"Oh no, no," Hilda says, her rosy cheeks turning grey, "Miss Perry is no longer with us."

"What?" I yelp.

Hilda's nostrils flare.

"She was insubordinate. Her skirts were unbecoming. She constantly mispronounced Caravaggio. She giggled all the way through your first tour last week which showed a lack of decorum."

My hands dangle at my sides. My jaw drops open. I can't blink. The girl of my dreams got fired because of my stupid jokes? How could this be any worse?

"But the final straw," Hilda continues, "was when I caught her in a compromising position in the cloakroom with that boyfriend of hers. Of course I had to terminate her employment then."

Jimmy got Zoe into a closet in the gallery? I feel like I might puke.

"Don't you worry, though, Mr. Sifter," Hilda says, resuming her sing-song voice. "I've hired a new girl to help you give the tours. I think you'll like her!"

In through the office door skips — no! It can't be!

"Good morning, Miss Hilda!" says my sister Charlotte, grinning smugly. "I'm all ready to start my first tour!"

"She's just as qualified as yourself, and I figured the two of you would work well together as a team, being siblings," Hilda beams.

"Yeah," Charlotte says, "and you'll be able to drive me back and forth to work, too!" She grins widely, relishing my suffering. "Won't that be fun, big brother?"

Charlotte turns to a reproduction on Hilda's office wall.

"Oh!" she squeals, "It's a Georgia O'Keefe! How beautiful!"

"Yes," Hilda smiles, "her work speaks to me."

"It speaks to me, too," Charlotte concurs.

Behind Hilda's desk hangs an old woodcut, which speaks to me. It's an illustration from Dante's *Inferno*, which shows a man being dragged down to hell.

Cheeseburger Subversive

(Grade twelve)

It has finally happened: My chance for redemption! Zoe Perry is sitting next to me on the squeaky, torn bench seat of my 1972 Ford pickup. Despite the size of the seat, she is pressed up against me, her cheek on my shoulder. Her position causes some difficulty when I have to shift gears, but hey, this is Zoe. Third gear will just have to wait.

This isn't a first date, exactly — Zoe and I were out on a date once in grade ten, but since it resulted in the engine of my car blowing up and in Zoe deciding to explore relationships with other guys, I've decided to look at this as a new beginning. And a major new beginning it is! Zoe is pressed up against me! Of her own free will! And all I had to do to get her here was manufacture a new personal ideology.

"It's supposed to be thirty-two degrees Celsius by noon," Zoe says. "The hottest day of the year so far!"

Indeed.

I softened her a little with a new-found knack for writing poetry, I softened her a little more with a new-found appreciation for art, and I warmed her nearly to the melting point by finding her jewellery when she lost it at the beach. I wanted so much for her to love me, I was beginning to fear that maybe she was too good for me. To think that I nearly blew it forever when I admitted, during one of our grade twelve political science classes, that, if I had been old enough to vote, I would have voted for the Conservatives in the last federal election. Zoe's look of disdain made me feel like crawling under my desk.

I suppose I should have known that Zoe had become a political *subversive*. I should have known it from her all black wardrobe, and from the dangling silver earrings shaped like the head of Karl Marx. While I was drawing doodles of airplanes and electric guitars in the margins of my notebook, Zoe was carefully carving slogans like *Question Authority before Authority questions You* across the top of her back row desk.

So, in my ignorance, I very nearly erased forever the possibility of having a torrid love affair with Zoe Perry. I blame it on the fact that she fooled me for years, first by wearing cute, pink jumpsuits and flowery sun dresses all through elementary school, then by wearing short skirts and tight jeans in grades nine and ten (which often caused me some major blood relocation). But more important, I blame nearly losing Zoe on my father.

My father votes Conservative. Always. Without question. "In our family," says Dad, almost threateningly, "we vote Conservative. My father voted Conservative, as did his father and grandfather, and his great grandfather, too." Dad even carries a blue-and-white card in his wallet that confirms his lifetime membership in the I-Vote-Conservative-No-Matter-What Club.

It was from my father that I got the impression that political subversives are all hunchbacked, gap-toothed, babbling homicidal maniacs. To my father, Charles

Manson is the type of guy who probably never voted Conservative. Subversives spend all of their time bombing police stations and belonging to clubs called fronts. They seldom bathe, wash their clothes, or shave. Dad says, "They're almost as destructive as the Liberal Party!"

So naturally, being raised to believe that conservatism is the major trait in normal-functioning brains, I was a little surprised when Zoe announced to everybody in class that she is an anarchist. She does wear black, of course, and she's got the earrings, but I was confused somewhat by her membership in the glee club and the prom committee. Also, quite unlike Charles Manson, she has a nice figure and exquisitely manicured nails. Her legs are slim, shaved, and generally very non-subversive looking.

"Anyone who votes Conservative votes against the working class!" she snapped.

Well, my dad is a working man (I think) so I was a little puzzled by her remark. At the same time, though, my heart was crushed.

How could I let politics triumph over love! I had to act quickly or lose her forever! Luckily, right before class, I had consumed two cans of Coke and three Ding Dongs at the local Quickie Mart, so my brain was spinning like the wheels of a supercharged Chevette.

"Well," I asserted boldly, "the bigger they are, the harder they fall, right? Since the pre-election polls indicated a landslide victory for the Conservatives anyway, I figured that the best strategy would be to help them win the election. That way, when we anarchists convince the rest of the country to rise against the government, the Conservative Party will be decimated in the process!"

Zoe's expression changed, which inspired me to continue. Summoning all I could remember from a Socialist Party of Canada leaflet that was once left under the windshield wiper of my truck, I jumped to my feet, my caffeine and sugar charged head buzzing, and chanted:

"Heck, give 'em all seats in the House of Commons! All the more Conservatives to fall on their big corporate butts when we pull the seats out from under them! And when the Conservatives fall, so shall the military-industrial complex! The strength will be sapped from the corporate stranglehold around the necks of the proletariat and the workers of our land will rise like a flood, cleansing all in their wake, washing away the sins of greed! So let 'em have the House of Commons! That way, they'll all be in one convenient location when we pull the green rug out from under them!"

The class was silent. I was out of breath. Zoe's eyes were glistening with tears. How could she have misjudged me so? Ah, the loquaciousness of love! The rhetoric of romance!

"Uh, yes, thank-you, Dak," muttered my astonished teacher. "A lovely speech, especially considering that your father holds a Progressive Conservative Party barbecue at your home each summer."

I wish he hadn't mentioned that.

"And yes," he says, "you are correct insofar as you point out that the rug of the House of Commons is indeed green. I'll give you a bonus mark if you can tell me what colour the Senate chamber is."

I was stumped. It could be meringue yellow for all I know. Nevertheless, Zoe met me at my locker after class.

"You were great in class today, Dak!" she says. "I'm sorry I was so short with you initially. I misunderstood you. Mr. Hawthorn was awestruck!"

Wow. *Awestruck!*

"I never would have guessed that you were an anarchist like me. I mean, I know you like poetry and art, but you wear pleated pants and loafers! You don't dress like a subversive at all! You part your hair on the right, too, which I always thought was supposed to be a subconscious confession of right-wing attitudes."

"Ah, but that's the idea, Zoe," I reply, trying to sound whiskey-smooth with my Coca-Cola voice. "Destroy the process from the inside. Act like one of them, dress like one of them, and they'll never know what hit 'em when we, the masses, turn on 'em."

"Wow," she says, "I hadn't considered *that* strategy before."

Okay, okay. I know that lying is wrong, and I have a nagging feeling that Zoe is smart enough to know that I don't really know any more about being a political subversive than I know about being a subatomic particle physicist. But I can't help it. I'm eighteen-years-old. I'm a man now, and I am subject to the dictatorship that biology holds over the higher morals of men. I seem to have Zoe's attention, and to keep it, I'm willing to undergo a philosophical transformation. Even if it means buying a black T-shirt.

"Would you like to go with me to a demonstration in Ottawa this weekend?" she bubbles. "It's a protest against killing animals for fur coats — like, I read about it in this underground magazine my dad got for me while he was in Toronto on a business trip. If it was in this magazine, there'll probably be about a million people show up, don't you think? I mean, we could wipe out the fur industry forever!"

Well, I personally don't have any special affinity for fur coats, since my mother has a mink that stinks like a skunk whenever it gets wet. Also, I think fur coats are overkill on anyone who isn't Sergeant Preston of the Yukon. This is a cause I could really support!

On the other hand, though, I've seen news footage of protesters getting hit by billy clubs, knocked down with water jets, and thrown into police cars by hairy armed cops. I'm not sure that the smell of wet fur offends me that much.

Nevertheless, I am hungry to know her better, to get beyond the physical attraction, and learn what makes her the way she is, so I accept her invitation.

"Can you drive?" she asks. "I'd drive myself, but Mom's got an I.O.D.E. meeting this weekend and Dad's got a golf game."

I agreed to drive, even though driving my octane-inhaling Ford tank all the way to Ottawa will cost me at least three weeks wages from J.D.'s Gas-O-Rama. It's worth it, though. I'm with Zoe, the most attractive woman in my political science class, perhaps in the entire world. Maybe, if we're lucky, we'll even get sprayed by a high-pressure water cannon together! Won't that be something to talk about in political science class! After all, Mr. Hawthorn is always telling us to get involved in the political process.

So, here we are, on our way to Ottawa.

"What's that weird noise?" Zoe asks, as we thunder along in the passing lane of Highway 401.

Despite the acute ideological embarrassment it causes Zoe, she has to admit that her mother drives an air-conditioned, leather-upholstered Saab, and her father rides around in a silver Mercedes the size of an aircraft carrier. The only sound Zoe is normally accustomed to hearing while riding inside a vehicle is the catatonic drone of her parents' Perry Como tapes.

"The noise — it's getting louder," she says. "Maybe we should pull over and look under the hood!"

I'm not sure which noise amid the cacophony is troubling her. There are so many from which to choose — the clattering of the valves, the hissing of the power steering pump, the buzzing of the alternator, the rumbling from the holes in the exhaust manifold, the clinking of the timing chain. The noises of proletarian conveyance.

"What does it sound like? Clatter? Hissing?"

"No," she says, cocking her head, "it's more of a whining sound — high pitched. Do you hear it?"

I listen through the din of mechanical breakdown for the noise she describes. Yes, she's right. A shrill new voice has joined the chorus.

"Yeah, I hear it," I say, "but I'm damned if I know what it is."

The whine becomes a shriek as we speed along.

"Maybe it's crying because it was due for retirement about a hundred thousand miles ago," I muse.

With that said, there is a loud thump, and the whining stops. Seconds later, the red TEMP light blinks on. With some situation-appropriate cursing, I slide the senile old truck onto the gravel at the side of the road.

As soon as I lift the hood, I see the problem. Hanging from an I-beam is the frayed remnant of what once served as a fan belt. I manage to limit my swearing to non-"F"-words, since Zoe is standing right beside me, peering into the under-hood cavern of doom.

"Fan belt," I say, gritting my teeth so hard they might shatter.

I tend to take it personally when my truck fails me. After all, I did pay two hundred dollars of my own hard-earned money for it! And I even fork over the cash for an oil change once a year! And this is the thanks I get!

I kick the bumper in a very subversive way. Zoe is gazing into the oil-blackened engine compartment, which radiates heat and chemical stench like the mouth of a volcano.

"Oh no. Look."

She points to the radiator that is peeing a steady green stream onto the ground.

Okay. Now I am going to lose my temper. I will scream, I will swear, I will jump around, and I will kick dents on top of the dents that already pock the surface of this stupid worthless truck! I am going to elevate the word tantrum to a whole new level of meaning!

Zoe, who is leaning on both palms against the front of the truck, looks up at me and does something completely out of place. Strands of her hair are hanging in her face, and she blows them away with a very gusty sigh. Then, oddly enough, she grins; a big, goofy grin.

It is as if she has reached inside me and snipped the right wire just nanoseconds before the explosion. Inexplicably, I find myself grinning, too.

She begins to laugh, shaking her head, her hair falling back into her face.

"What are the odds of these two problems happening at exactly the same moment?" she says, practically choking on laughter.

I find myself laughing along with her. It is like being towed out of quicksand.

I think I am in love with her. For Zoe, I would definitely commit an act of subversion against the military-industrial complex! Even if I'm not sure which city it's in! Even if it resulted in losing my driver's licence! I would do it for her!

No other woman has ever caused this many exclamation marks to appear in my thoughts! I'm so inspired by her presence that I think I'll start ranting!

"It's a damned conspiracy against the working man, I tell you! Who drives trucks? Corporate executives? No! The working man, that's who! It's a plot to keep the proletariat immobile!"

I kick the side of the truck just for effect. I kick it so hard that I throw myself off balance, twisting my ankle in the process. Is a pronounced limp considered subversive-looking? I hope so.

"Wait!" Zoe yelps, "I've got it!"

"Got what?"

"They taught us in home ec that you can use a pair of pantyhose as a temporary fan belt!"

"Really?"

"Really. I'm not kidding."

A miracle! Her own legs are sheathed in fan-belt black, with exactly the material we need to make the repair! It is surely the first time I have stared lustily at a girl's legs with intentions of auto repair. We're saved! What a stroke of luck! We will not miss the revolution for lack of transportation!

"Well?" she says.

"Well what? Let's fix the stupid thing and get back on the road!"

"First you're going to have to turn around so I can take these off."

I'm not sure if the expression on her face is one of genuine modesty or of calculated coyness. My female-expression-decoding-system is not very well calibrated. I haven't been a man for very long, after all.

"Oh yeah," I grunt. "Sorry."

I spin around on my heel, the one which isn't throbbing with pain. The sun is hovering just above the treeline, directly behind me. Zoe is behind me as well, just to my left. Her shadow stretches casually in front of me, sprawling out on the surface of the highway like a slender house cat. I am trying SO hard to ignore it, to remain true to my mission to ignore her physical attributes for a while and get to know Zoe better as a person, but dammit! It's difficult to stop the blood from migrating south as I watch Zoe's shadow-shorts descend the length of her shadow-legs, and as she peels the nylons from her long, two-dimensional leg-shadows. I see her shadow bend over into an elongated arc, and I watch the shorts shimmy back up her shadow-legs into position around her waist.

Is it immoral to watch the shadow of a girl removing her shorts? Is it wrong to picture in one's mind what the actual girl at the other end of the shadow might look like beneath the black drapery? In the space between my eyes I can see her, all milky-white, smooth and beautiful.

I'm sure my father would tell me that I am being immoral right now. My sister Charlotte would tell me I'm being a P.I.G. — a Pitiful, Ignorant Guy. Parts of my body are quite suddenly acting very subversive. A definite uprising is underway! My new black jeans are even less comfortable than they were moments earlier.

"Okay, I'm done," she says. "You can turn around now."

I hope my subversion isn't showing too much.

She tosses the pantyhose at me. I run the former leggings around the alternator, pump, and fan pulleys, and I tie a knot in the rigging. If only installing a real fan belt was this easy!

"There!" I grunt, slapping my hands together to shake loose the dirt (It's a hormonal law that a man must do this every time he touches anything under the hood of a vehicle).

"Now, what are we going to do about this damned radiator leak?" I had meant the question to be rhetorical, but Zoe supplies an answer.

"Well, in home ec they told us that if you put a teaspoon of pepper into a radiator, it will seal any small leaks. For a while, anyway."

"Get outta here!"

"Seriously!" she explains, "the grains of pepper get pushed into the hole by the circulating radiator fluid, and then the hot water in the radiator makes the pepper expand to seal the leak."

Why did I take auto shop instead of home ec? All we learned in shop was how to accurately throw S.A.E. sockets at each other, and how to install new tires on the shop teacher's Buick Skylark.

"There's a McDonald's at the next service station, I think," says Zoe, who is forcing me to love her more and more by the minute. "I hope we have enough water left in the rad to get us there."

"There's one way to find out!" I say.

I reach for the cap on the radiator and give it a hearty twist.

Angry, hissing green water explodes skyward. The radiator cap hurtles somewhere into the upper stratosphere. Hot water surges Old Faithful-style, blasting against my chest. The volcanic discharge knocks me onto my back.

I roll around frantically in the roadside gravel, screaming things like "Ooo-ooo-ooo! Eee-eee-eee!" and other manly utterances. I tear off my steaming black shirt and throw it on the ground. I jump to my feet and prance up and down on the shirt until it has become a shredded, mucky component of the roadway.

"Are . . . you . . . okay?" Zoe gasps, as I finally stop gyrating and slump against the driver's side door.

"Uhh . . . I think so."

I feel as if a nuclear warhead has just passed through my torso, but I have only a red patch on my skin to show for my suffering.

"You *sure* you're okay?" Zoe asks again.

"Yeah. I'm okay."

She lets out a shaky sigh, followed by a stifled giggle. "Your burn is shaped like Whistler's Mother!"

Under normal circumstances, a man is hormonally required to get very pouty when a woman giggles at his injuries. But this is Zoe, the most attractive woman in the universe, so I let it slide.

I retrieve the rad cap from where it has landed, and return it to its benevolent position atop the radiator.

"If this old engine overheats and explodes, we'll just have to think of it as a mercy killing!" I say.

Against all odds, the pickup sputters all the way to McDonald's without further incident. I'm in as much danger of exploding as the old truck, since I have been holding my breath for the last few kilometers.

"I have to use the washroom," Zoe says matter-of-factly. "I'll meet you out here by the picnic tables. You go and get some pepper and some water for the radiator. And some food, if you don't mind. I don't know about you, but I'm starving!"

Perhaps not coincidentally, I am also very hungry. We are becoming soulmates, I think! When Zoe is hungry, I am hungry, too!

My momentarily restored spirit plunges again into darkness, though, as I plod into McDonald's. Apparently, every human being within a hundred-mile radius has simultaneously felt a craving for a Big Mac. A chain of humanity twists like a heat-dazed snake all the way from the entrance to the serving counter. Six or seven recent graduates of puberty race back and forth behind the counter, haplessly attempting to appease the burger-starved masses.

A hand-lettered cardboard sign above the menu board offers an apologetic explanation for the droplets of sweat that congregate on my forehead:

OUR AIR CONDITIONER IS TEMPERARILY BROKE. SORRY FOR THE ~~INCONVEEN~~ TROUBLE!

A fat guy stands directly in front of me, gushing rank sweat from every fold and orifice. He wears a faded tank top, has tattoos on his forearms and thick, curly hair on his enormous shoulders. He utters goddamn every few seconds. He is the kind of guy you often see mulling about in back road junkyards. I hope that if, God forbid, he decides to hurt someone, it isn't me.

"What's taking so goddamn long?" he hollers. "Goddamn this heat! Goddamn this lineup!" He enunciates each goddamn in a way that makes me wonder whether or not God actually has damned this restaurant to the flames of hell. It's certainly beginning to feel that way. Sweat is stinging my eyes.

I stand at the tail of this writhing human python as it slowly slithers towards the counter. More people have packed in behind me. Inescapably bright images of fun ol' Ronald McDonald and his happy McDonaldland buddies imbed themselves on my retinas. My stomach growls in agony, twisting as if it's hooked up to some medieval torturing device. Heat, hunger, and my newly acquired subversive attitude are beginning to overtake me. I am on the verge of irrational behaviour.

The proliferation of "goddamns" in the general buzz of conversation is increasing at an alarming rate. Someone shouts: "The goddamned drinks should be free, it's so goddamned hot in this place!" Voices from other spots in the line grunt in agreement.

Tempers rise. The greasy smell of mutiny saturates the air beneath the Golden Arches. Terminally McHappy carnival colours slash at my senses from all directions. In tiny lettering at the bottom of a large picture of Ronald and the Gang, I read: "The names and likenesses of McDonaldland characters are registered trademarks of the McDonald's Corporation." Corporation!

A-*ha*! So this is a corporate conspiracy!

Through the humid haze, I see a frantic fourteen-year-old struggling with a stubborn milkshake machine. There is a loud popping noise, then pink, syrupy goo spits out in all directions.

The teen hollers several *awshits* before finally disabling the spewing beast by pulling its plug. Covered in a sticky mess, the kid yelps, "Sorry folks, shake machine's busted!" and retreats into the white-tiled void behind the counter.

Under normal circumstances, this would been a moment of classic hilarity. The tension would have been broken. Everybody would have shared a laugh at the kid's expense.

But no one cracks a smile. Everyone stands like statues, arms folded. The fat guy with the furry shoulders starts hollering.

"No shakes! No shakes! I been waitin' here for half an hour! I wanna fuckin' shake! I wanna fuckin' shake!"

This is certainly a sign that things are about to spin out of control. The fat guy's goddamns have turned into fuckin's. This is not good.

Surprisingly, the fat guy's order (four cheeseburgers, a large fry, and oddly enough, a large hot coffee) is delivered without any major incident. If anything had been wrong with his order, there would have been certain chaos. Revolution would have been unstoppable.

The kid behind the cash register crosses his arms across the front of his blue-and-white striped polyester uniform. "Have a nice day!" he oozes, as if he truly believes that the fat guy's mood can be salvaged by his happy-ass McDonald's customer-manipulation training.

The counter boy grins cockily, having bravely protected McDonaldland from certain pandemonium with his diplomacy.

"Next!" he croons, tipping his triangular paper cap forward like a cowboy hat. After that near miss, he feels sure that he can take on anything that comes his way.

He is wrong. I am next in line, and I am feeling subversive like I've never felt before.

"Hi," I say, grinning like I'm trying out for the part of Alex in a stage production of *A Clockwork Orange*.

"I'd like, um, several Big Macs, a few large, frosty beverages of some kind, many many crispy golden fries — "

The kid behind the counter raises his hand in the air like a harried traffic cop.

"I'm sorry, sir, but I can't serve you. Our rules do not permit us to serve customers who are not wearing a shirt or shoes."

I look down at my chest. Oops, no shirt. I forgot about that.

"But, but," I stammer, grinning stupidly, eyes bulging, "I'm wearing shoes!"

The kid looks at me with the warmth and compassion of a constipated Gestapo officer.

"I am going to have to ask you to leave, sir."

My sensibilities are trickling away.

"Aw listen kid. I've had a rotten day today . . . "

I grope desperately for something that will convince him that it is his humanitarian duty to serve me. Suddenly, miraculously, my mental soundtrack fires up an old TV commercial jingle I heard when I was very young.

"Listen, buddy, remember back to about 1981, when the McDonald's slogan was 'You Deserve A Break Today?'"

I am greeted with a Tabula Raisa face.

"Well, uh, couldn't you give me a break today? Just this once? Please?"

"Sir," he gasps, "the rules are the rules. I can't serve you because you aren't wearing a shirt. If you were wearing a shirt, I would be happy to give you a break. But you aren't wearing a shirt, are you? So please step aside."

I began to feel delirious. All the McHappy colours began to close in on me. Surely he would take pity on me if he understood the circumstances!

"But, I can explain! The fan belt in the truck broke, and Zoe took off her pantyhose, but then the radiator exploded on me, and I threw my shirt on the ground so it wouldn't burn me, and by the time I finished jumping on it, it was full of gravel!"

"Please, sir," he moans, looking at me as if I am something a mongrel has just thrown up, "I don't want to have you thrown out, but the rules are the rules."

Who the hell does this little twerp think he is? Mayor McCheese's top deputy? Chief Magistrate of the McDonaldland Justice Department?

"Listen, Captain Hamburger, you had better take my order," my voice becomes a shriek, "or else I am going to cause a commotion! You hear me? A commotion!"

He stares at me like McDonaldland's own *Dirty Harry*.

"Either get a shirt on or get out of here, asshole!"

As soon as the word asshole leaves his lips, I spin around to face the waiting crowd.

"Did you hear that? Did you hear that?" I scream at my comrades in the long lineup. "This Nazi Youth tells me that he won't serve me because, God forbid, you have to have a shirt on to be served! Even if it is hot enough in here to fry a cheeseburger on your own forehead!"

The crowd gasps in collective empathy.

Ha! Not so cocky now are you, thou zit-faced pawn of the corporate elite! Step up and feel the wrath of the masses, thou servant of evil masters!

The kid pleads desperately with the rumbling crowd.

"Listen! It's not my fault it's hot in here! I'd like to serve this guy, but he has to be wearing a shirt! There's nothing I can do! They could fire me!"

Using reason on this crowd, though, is about as useful as trying to drive ants away from a picnic basket by throwing sugar at them.

"C'mon, junior," comes a voice from the rising din, "give the guy a break!"

"Yeah!" says another.

The kid must have been the top graduate at the McDonaldland Academy, because he refuses to give in.

With courage that would make Ronald McDonald flush with pride, he suddenly starts screaming while waving a drink dispensing nozzle in the air.

"Listen, pal," he hollers, "either you get your ass out of this restaurant, or you're gonna get it!"

"Get what?" I cackle menacingly, my face hovering inches from his.

"Get *this*, shithead!"

Before I can retreat he blasts me in the face with the dispensing nozzle.

"Aaaaaaugh!" I yelp, frenzied and helpless (If you have ever had a pressurized stream of root beer shot directly into your eyes, you will understand my reaction).

My feet lose traction in the slick of soda, and I hit the floor with an awful slap, but only after careening off a life-sized statue of Ronald's pal Grimace (Grimace, as you will recall, is the McDonaldland character who looks like a globular purple fungus).

"Next!" howls the crazed counter boy, still gripping the dispenser nozzle, a stream of fizzing ammunition trickling down his forearm into the sleeve of his uniform.

Several other customers rush to their fallen comrade, me. Unfortunately for peace and order, I have unwittingly landed atop a pile of ketchup packets.

"Good Lord!" a woman shrieks, "he's bleeding!"

"No, no, It's only ketchup. I'm okay," I try to say, but what actually escapes from my mouth is an unintelligible gurgle, since my lungs are half-filled with foaming root beer.

It's too late to start preaching peace anyhow. The fat guy with the ugly temper jumps atop a garbage box, tears off his tank top, and hollers, "Look, no shirt! Look, no shirt! Gonna take my food away? Huh? Huh? Gonna take away my hamburger! Huh? Ya gonna?"

Others in the crowd start removing their shirts as well, as a show of solidarity I suppose. Karl Marx would have loved every minute of this, but I just want out.

Beer-bellies swing forth unrestrained; sweat-stained T-shirts cut circles through the air like helicopter blades; ketchup and vinegar packets pop like revolutionary pistols. A couple of women, to ensure that the cause of women's equality is not lost in the fray, remove their shirts — a development that certainly does not go unnoticed.

I drag my ketchup and pop-stained body towards the exit door. I have become a symbol for the burger-starved masses, a figurehead in what will surely rank right up there with the Upper Canada Rebellion in future editions of The Canadian History Book. I have just caused the McDonaldland Mutiny.

A good, hard smack in the head, courtesy of the tile floor, has delivered my brain back from its heat-inspired vacation. My strongest instinct now is to get as far away from here as possible before the police arrive with tear gas and billy clubs, looking for the guy who started it all.

A pail-sized cup of Sprite lands on the floor in front of me. I grab it, for use as surrogate radiator fluid. I also snatch a few packets of pepper.

Zoe is sitting on a plastic picnic table outside.
"My God!" she cries, "what happened to you?"

"There was an uprising. I got shot in the eyes with root beer."

"What do you mean, an uprising?"

"Some maniac went berserk from the heat. He started ranting and raving, and pretty soon the whole crowd went nuts! It was crazy! I thought I'd be killed!"

Okay, so I misrepresented the facts somewhat, but I'm afraid that the uprising I have just created is not exactly the kind of subversive activity that turns on girls. I have bent the truth yet again. Biology is warping my morals. The fact that Zoe now has her arms around me is just accelerating my moral decline.

"My God! How awful!" cries Zoe. "People can be such animals!"

We decide to skip the anti-fur rally, considering that we've just narrowly escaped an ugly insurrection. Also, neither of us is sure that my truck will make it all the way to Ottawa in one piece.

We go to a Disney movie instead, and, as we leave the theatre, we both agree that it was very cute and amusing, despite the fact that the Disney corporation is one of the richest on the planet. After the movie, while sitting under the stars, kissing each other in the open box of my truck in the middle of an empty parking lot, I ask Zoe if she'll go to the prom with me.

She says yes.

We're going to rent a stretch limousine for the occasion, and Zoe is going to buy a white satin dress with pink lace and white gloves. I'm renting a tux with a top hat and cane.

We are not abandoning our subversive ideals, though. We're not going to clap when our principal gives his dinner speech, and we're both going to wear black sunglasses.

Long live the revolution!

Tristan's Quarter
(First-year, university)

This is the dorm room where I live. The skinny guy lying on the more neatly made bed is my roommate, Tristan. I am deeply concerned about him.

Beside his bed he's got a copy of *The Complete Works of Shakespeare*. You can tell by the unbroken spine that he has never actually opened it, but he keeps it near his bed just in case he ever needs it.

"Shakespeare impresses chicks," he once told me. "My brother says that every guy should have Shakespeare on his shelf just so he can hold his own."

If you want to know the truth, though, holding his own is about all the action Tristan ever gets. To the best of my knowledge, Tristan has never brought a female back to the dorm room we share. Come to think of it, I've never actually witnessed a conversation between Tristan and *any* female which has lasted for more than a few syllables. I think he once mentioned having a girlfriend in high school, but he's never said anything about her since.

Tristan keeps nine hundred or so comic books hidden beneath his bed. There's a Captain Kirk uniform in his closet. He has highly animated debates with himself. It is not these little idiosyncrasies, though, but something else which has made me begin to worry about Tristan:

he believes that he can find the answers to the most pressing questions of destiny by merely flipping a quarter.

"You've got to understand the principles of quantum mechanics and synchronicity," he explains, "to understand how the seemingly random act of tossing a coin into the air can be used to predict one's future. The motion of all objects, spaces, ideas, and emotions are interconnected, you see. A tossed coin can land with only two results: Heads up, or tails up . . . "

"What if the coin lands on its edge?" I ask.

"Don't be difficult, Dak. The uncertainty principle would account for that unlikely possibility. May I continue?"

I shrug. It's fairly obvious to even a scientific illiterate like myself that Tristan has gleaned his data about the interconnected nature of time, space, and destiny more from sci-fi comic books than from anything by Stephen Hawking or Carl Jung.

"All right then," he continues, oblivious to the rolling of my eyes. "A coin can either land heads up, or tails up. Only two possible results. A question which is posed in such a way as to elicit only a yes or no response can produce only one of two answers. Therefore, the variability affecting both incidents is equal, and as such, there is a meaningful connection established between the two events."

I ask him: "What if the answer to your question is maybe?"

"The answer, dear Dak, can *never* be *maybe*."

I pull a quarter from my pocket.

"Let's test your theory, Tristan. Heads, you're psychotic maniac. Tails, you're a drooling retard."

I flick the coin from my thumb. It defects off Tristan's forehead and disappears through the heating grate on the floor. Oops!

Tristan sighs.

"You never take me seriously."

A few days later I catch Tristan practicing his unusual personal religion. He is asking questions, it seems, to the tiled ceiling of our dorm room, while flipping a coin onto his bed. He says each word slowly, deliberately, as if English is the ceiling's second language. I watch with both horror and amusement through the crack I have opened in the door.

"Does she love me?" he intones.

The quarter lands tails up on his neatly made bed. He looks disappointed.

"Okay then, is she in love with me?"

Tails again. He snatches the coin from the bed and tries again.

"Is she *falling* in love with me?"

Tails.

"Will she *probably* fall in love with me in the *very near future*?"

This time, the coin comes up heads.

"Ya-hoooo! She's going to fall in love with me! It's going to happen!"

He dances around like somebody has just tested jumper cables on his privates.

A-HA! This explains everything! Perhaps Tristan isn't a complete lunatic after all. He's IN LOVE!

"Hi, Tristan!" I bark happily as I shove the door open and throw my knapsack onto my bed.

He stops immediately, frozen in an unnatural position like a mannequin at a lingerie boutique.

"Cajoling the predictive forces of the time-space continuum, were you?" I ask.

"Whadda you mean?"

"So," I ask, grinning, "if you ask the forces of the universe the same question enough times, do they eventually get fed up and give you what you want?"

Tristan does not laugh.

"Don't be a jerk, Dak. I asked a *different* question each time. You've got to ask very specific questions because you can only get a yes-or-no answer. There's a difference between *loving* someone, *being in love* with someone, *falling in love,* and being *about to fall* in love!"

He slumps onto his bed, and buries his face in his pillow.

"What can I do?" comes his muffled cry. "What can I do to make her fall in love with me sooner? I can't wait forever!"

Poor Tristan. I feel bad for him. I've been through this sort of hell before, too.

"What's her name, Tris?" I ask sympathetically.

"Her name is Veronica."

Veronica, eh? The name of a *comic book* girl, if I'm not mistaken — the type of comic book girl with anatomically impossible breasts. If I remember correctly, she dates a comic book dork named Archie, a character with whom Tristan shares more than a few physical characteristics. Interesting . . .

"Does she know you like her?" I ask.

"Like her? I *love* her! I hear her voice in gurgling tap water! Cracks in the pavement spell out her name! I see her face in the bark of trees!"

"Um, you told her all of that?"

"Everything."

"What, um, did she think of all of that?" I ask, while wondering if she has called the police yet.

He sighs.

"She says she thinks I'm cute."

"Well, that's a good sign, I suppose . . . "

Tristan frowns.

"There's a major problem: she's already in love with another guy."

"Oh, come on, Tristan!" I say, "I'm sure he's no match for you!"

He sighs again. It is becoming a reflexive action for him, like blinking or breathing.

"She's in love with Kurt Cobain," he mutters.

"The dead rock star?"

"The same."

Oh dear. This IS bad news for my batty roommate. Dead rock stars are pretty tough competition because they do not tend to make the same clumsy mistakes which we living men are inclined to commit, such as jokingly referring to a girlfriend's special prom night hairdo as *Eva Braun-esque*. Or backing a girlfriend's father's Lincoln Continental into Sammy's Souvlaki Hut. Or projectile-vomiting on a girlfriend's prom dress after delivering a lengthy speech on one's masculine ability to stomach great quantities of cheap contraband liquor. But I digress. This is Tristan's story, not mine.

"Love is hell," moans Tristan, pounding a fist against his pillow.

"Buck up, Tristan!" I heartily bark, "there are plenty of fish in the sea!"

These were the exact words of wisdom delivered to me by my father on the night Zoe dumped me. Unfortunately, they are as calming to Tristan as they were to me.

"I don't want any other fish! I want Veronica!" he wails, "She's the only fish for me!"

Four days have passed since Tristan's revelation of undying love, and I have acquired a headache at least as intense as the pain in Tristan's heart. Perhaps the throbbing in my brain has been caused by the lack of sleep resulting from the ghastly three AM shrieks of "Oh, Veronica!" There is also the possibility that in some subconscious way, I empathize with Tristan's predicament. Whatever the reason, I have become determined to help Tristan win the hand of his wayward beauty before he dies of heartache (or strangulation).

There is only one problem: I am not exactly a Rhodes Scholar on the subject of what attracts women to men. After mulling the issue over thoroughly in my mind (and having consumed three cans of Guinness), I decide to go right to the source: I will ask an actual woman! Specifically, I will call my ex-girlfriend Zoe.

Maybe, somehow, my wanting to help another person will warm her heart, and maybe she will forgive me for what happened. And maybe if I flap my arms hard enough, I'll be able to fly to the moon. But, anything is worth a try. I would rather know that she is completely finished with me and get all the misery over with at once, rather than clinging to the faint hope of reconciliation for the next four years of living on the same campus. I wonder if she enrolled at the same university just to torture me.

So now I am holding the receiver of a pay phone against my cheek. My throat is dry. The phone on the other end of the line rings four times, then there is a click, followed by short, quiet hum. Damn. It's her answering machine.

"Hi there!" says Zoe's recorded voice. "I'm not able to take your call right now but please leave a message. Unless this is Dak, in which case you can hang up immediately. And never call me again. You prick."

Beep.

"Zoe! Listen to this message! Please please please! I really, desperately need your help! This is not another scheme to get you to be my girlfriend again, I promise! The happiness of another human being is at stake here. My roommate is in a desperate situation! I can't save him without your help!"

I am about to hang up when I think to add something.

"Please, help us, Obi-Wan. You're our only hope."

I am hoping that this quotation from *Star Wars* will soften her a little. I used to do it all the time when we were in high school. She thought it was cute. Well, at the time, anyway.

The phone line continues to hum indifferently. Maybe this wasn't such a good idea. I am such a buffoon. I'm just about to hang up when Zoe's voice (the real live version) comes through the receiver.

"This had better be good, Dak."

When I am finished explaining the situation to her, there is a protracted silence.

"Okay," she says finally, "I'll try to help you with this guy. But I'm not making any promises."

"Aw, thanks, Zoe!" I gush, "you can't imagine what this means to me. I love you for doing this! I could kiss you!"

"It'll be a cold day in hell before you ever kiss me again, Dak."

"Sorry," I say. "Will you still help me?"

"I'll meet you at the Elbow Room at 8:30. You can buy me a drink and we'll talk about it."

She hangs up.

It is nearly midnight. Tristan, Zoe, and I are huddled around a table at the Elbow Room. Tristan and Zoe have been discussing in great detail the things a man should do and *not* do when pursuing a potential mate. My role in all of this has been to keep quiet, pay for the drinks, and to accept an occasional cold glance from Zoe whenever she mentions one of the things a man should *not* do.

"Thanks, Zoe," says Tristan, his chest swelling, "I'm ready to go claim Veronica as my own!"

She shakes her head.

"No, Tristan. Nobody can *claim* anyone else. All you can do is offer yourself, and hope that the other person accepts."

He deflates.

"What if she *doesn't accept*? I'll die!"

"Well, if you really like her that much, try again. You might endear yourself to her."

"Does that really work?" I pipe in.

"Not in *your* case," she says.

Tristan digs a quarter from his pocket. He looks up at the smoke-yellowed barroom ceiling.

"Will Veronica be mine by the end of this evening?" he moans like a magician uttering an incantation.

He flips the quarter into the air. It lands with a plop in my half-drained beer glass. He grabs my beer and peers into it with one eye.

"Yes! It's heads! Yes!"

Tristan goes prancing out of the bar like a kid in a playground who has just won the big marble. Zoe is smiling.

"Boy, you weren't exaggerating! He's absolutely mental!"

Zoe has a wonderful smile. I'm staring at her. I can't help it.

"Stop it, Dak," she says quietly. "Don't look at me like that."

So I stare at the quarter at the bottom of my glass, only sneaking a couple of glances at her when she isn't looking. That harvest-time wheat coloured hair of hers is longer than ever. It's pulled back in a pony tail revealing her perfect cheekbones, her cute little nose. God. She's a full-grown woman. She's beautiful. She's amazing. And I'm an idiot.

My brain works furiously on how to deal with this crushing silence. Jokes? No, she's too angry with me. Charm? Ha. Good one. Send flowers? Get real. You're in a bar, stupid! Besides, it's far too late for flowers.

My eyes are flitting desperately around the room now, looking for any diversion to end this quiet hell. But just as I feel like I might implode, a dozen or so young women wearing black W.I.C. T-shirts march through the entrance to the Elbow Room. A few of them are carrying signs, hand-lettered with such slogans as *Pornography Equals Disrespect!* and *Shame on Speaker's Corner!* Yes! The diversion I was hoping for!

W.I.C. stands for Women's Issues Commission, and the issue in question, of course, is the sale of *Playboy* from the racks of Speaker's Corner, the overpriced convenience store located in the basement of the university community centre. Apparently, the W.I.C.s (who seem to be mostly sociology majors) think that the sale of soft-core pornography within the hallowed walls of an academic institution is wrong. Fair enough, I think. Can you imagine what Tristan would be like if, instead of anatomically ridiculous comic book illustrations of women, he had access to nude photos of real women? They'd have to cart him away in a white truck!

The W.I.C. protesters have procured a large table near the bar. They have ordered a tray of draught beer; apparently, temperance is not part of their mandate. I like them already! Also, contrary to the stereotypes perpetuated by *The Bolt* (the underground newspaper run by mostly male engineering students), the majority of the protesters are cute, perky-looking undergraduates. Some of them wear makeup, and those in skirts possess recently shaved legs: hobby protestors!

The presence of the W.I.C.s does not present a sufficient diversion in itself, though. However, six male engineering students have entered the bar directly behind the W.I.C.s, wearing Hugh Hefner-style smoking jackets. They are singing the engineering student theme song, which goes:

"We are, we are, we are, we are, we are the engineers
We can, we can, we can, we can demolish forty beers!"

"How?" I wonder aloud. "By dropping the bottles out a fifth-storey window?"

Zoe resists the urge to laugh.

The engineering students have positioned themselves at a table adjacent to the young female protesters.

"Hey, boys!" hollers the loudest of the engineers, "you know what 'W.I.C.' stands for? 'Wish I had a cock!'"

Three of the his colleagues erupt into laughter; the other two cover their faces with their hands and shake their heads.

A thin, pretty, black-haired girl at the W.I.C. table turns towards the Hefners and says, "Then I guess you boys should join up, eh?"

Ooh! Good one! I'll have to give her two points for that. Hefners – 1, W.I.C.s – 2!

"Hey, baby," snorts the head Hefner, "that was a pretty good one for somebody who is against the freedom of expression!"

Uh oh. I don't like the direction this is heading.

"First of all," says the black-haired woman, "the term 'baby' really doesn't apply to anyone over the age of two. But never mind that. Can I ask you a personal question?"

"Fire away!" says the guy.

"Suppose you got drunk and passed out here, then I stripped you naked, stuck a cucumber up your ass, took a picture of you, and then pinned copies of it on the walls all over campus. Would that be okay? Would I be free to express myself in that way?"

The head Hefner steps towards her.

"I liked the part about you stripping me naked!"

"Dream on, asshole," she replies.

"Veronica!" comes a voice from the other side of the bar.

It's Tristan. He sprints through the room toward the black-haired debater.

This is the girl Tristan has gone mental over? This is Veronica? Wow. Tristan suddenly seems more real to me.

Veronica looks at Tristan. Her expression mellows.

"Hi, Tris."

"I called your place, and your roommate said I might find you here."

His expression turns to panic.

"Hey. Who's *this* guy?"

The Hefner wannabe smirks.

"Hey, babe, it's no wonder you don't like men, if *this* friggin' geek's your boyfriend!"

"I'd like to be!" says Tristan.

"He's got a better chance than you do, jerk!" Veronica barks.

"I do?" coos Tristan.

"Aw! She must be a lesbian!" says the guy too loudly. His compatriots no longer seem to find any of this very amusing. Dressing up in funny outfits and drinking beer is one thing, but demeaning cute young women — potential *dates* is not what they had in mind.

"Yup," says Mr. Charming, "I think she's a rug-muncher!"

Veronica flushes. She glares at her nemesis, throws her arms around Tristan, and locks onto his face with one of the most vacuum-intensive kisses I have ever witnessed.

When she finally pulls herself away, Tristan is cross-eyed with elation. Veronica wears a tight-lipped smile.

"Wrong guess, asshole," she says to Mr. Charming.

"Bitch!" he spits.

Tristan's expression blanks, and he does something that approaches the Humphrey Bogart level of coolness. I am totally amazed — maybe he *has* learned something from all those comic books!

"Wrong again, buddy," he says. "That's zero out of two. Shall we try for three?"

He launches a fist in the direction of his beloved's nemesis. *Tres cool*, Tristan!

Unfortunately, his aim is poor and his punch glances off the guy's shoulder. Mr. Charming socks Tristan in the eye, sending him crashing into an onlooker's table.

What the hell am *I* doing? I'm on my feet. I'm sprinting towards Mr. Charming. I've got him by the shoulders. I've spun him around. I've got his arms behind his back. I'm pushing him towards the door.

Where did I learn *this* stuff?

"Out!" I bark, as I launch him through the door, his ass via my foot.

Back at the other side of the bar, the remaining engineers are apologizing profusely to the more attractive members of the W.I.C. contingent. Veronica and Tristan are now sitting together in a dark corner. She is dabbing at his eye with an ice cube. Tristan wears the expression of a heaven-bound soul.

"I thought you were in love with Kurt Cobain?" Tristan sighs.

"Only in theory, Tristan," Veronica says.

Zoe joins me at the exit.

"Your lip is bleeding," she says.

I touch my fingers to my lip. Yep, it's blood.

"Geeze, I hate violence," I gripe.

"Except at hockey games, right?" Zoe says.

"I'm not so crazy about it when it involves me personally."

Instinctively, I put on my Don Cherry impersonation voice.

"Let this be a lesson to all you kids out there — keep those sticks down!"

Zoe's face. Is she grinning? Yes, I'm sure of it. A grin! But now it's gone.

"Well," she says.

"Well," I reply.

"See you later, I guess . . . "

She turns, pushes the crash bar of the exit door, and she's gone.

I nearly follow her but it occurs to me that Mr. Charming could still be out there waiting to put my teeth into my digestive regions. I opt for the back door.

I catch Tristan's eye as I pass. He gives me the thumbs-up sign as Veronica whispers in his ear.

I sit on the curb behind the Elbow Room, leaning against a plump garbage bag. I'm thinking about the Valentine card I made for Zoe in grade six. On the back of it I wrote, "I want to be Han Solo to your Princess Leia," then I promptly ripped it up to avoid being taunted by the other boys at school. I'm thinking about our first car date, when I blew up the engine in my doomed old Pontiac trying to race a guy in a Camaro.

I'm thinking about when we used her pantyhose to fix my old Ford truck. I'm thinking about how she wiped root beer from my eyes after my *disagreement* with a McDonald's counter boy last year, and about how she wiped blood off my lip after I got punched on the school bus in grade six. I'm thinking about the time in grade eleven, when she wasn't speaking to me, and I wrote a poem for her and read it out loud in class and didn't care if anyone laughed. I'm thinking about how I discovered later that she retrieved that poem from the classroom garbage, smoothed it out, and put it in a pewter frame on her bedside table.

Most of all, I'm thinking about the first time I kissed her, how her lips felt so perfectly warm, like waking in a pool of sunshine through a window pane on a summer morning. I remember how her lips tasted like a strawberry milkshake, how her hair smelled fresh like a forest after a late spring rain. One complex feeling kept crashing over me like a wave as her lips touched mine: *You care about people, you are thoughtful and kind, you are forgiving, and you are so much more than the pretty face and body that initially attracted me to you. You are smarter, wiser, stronger, and braver than I. You are light years ahead of me. I love you, Zoe Perry.*

And this is the thought that finally breaks the dam and lets the tears flow, and I don't even give a shit that I look like a pathetic drunken loser, crying and sitting on a pile of garbage in an alley behind a bar.

"Cruddy night, buddy?" mumbles a drunk who has wandered into the alley (He must be a closet poet, too).

"You doan look so good, pal," he says as he passes. "Here. Call yerself a cab."

A quarter clinks before me on the sidewalk. Right.

I try to ignore it.

Oh, what the hell. I toss the quarter. It lands on the pavement, heads up.

Mere chance. I toss it again.

Heads.

And again.

Heads.

Should I go after Zoe?

Heads.

If I were to tell her that I really am sorry, that I feel terrible about what I did, that I really, really miss her and would do practically anything to get her back, will she forgive me?

Heads.

Can I catch her if I run?

Heads.

I know this is crazy, I know I should be locked away in a padded room somewhere . . .

but I'm running.